My Daughter's Wedding

Also by Claire Baldry

Poetry Booklets
Simply Bexhill
Simply Christmas
The De La Warr Date
Seaside and Sailaway
Simply Modern Life

Autobiographical Novella
South Something

Debut Novel
Different Genes

MY DAUGHTER'S WEDDING

Claire Baldry

Matador
9 Priory Business Park,
Wistow Road, Kibworth Beauchamp,
Leicestershire. LE8 0RX
Tel: 0116 279 2299
Email: books@troubador.co.uk
Web: www.troubador.co.uk/matador
Twitter: @matadorbooks

ISBN 978 1838590 338

British Library Cataloguing in Publication Data.
A catalogue record for this book is available from the British Library.

Printed and bound by CPI Group (UK) Ltd, Croydon, CR0 4YY
Typeset in 11pt Bembo by Troubador Publishing Ltd, Leicester, UK

Matador is an imprint of Troubador Publishing Ltd

For Emily and Mike

NOTE FROM THE AUTHOR

I have undertaken the role of 'mother of the bride' twice now. In both instances at least some of the major participants (including myself) had been divorced, remarried or were living with new partners. I am part of a 'modern' family.

This novel is entirely fictional, and none of the characters are based on people I know. However, my experience as 'mother of the bride' has given me an insight into some of the complications which can arise when organising a wedding within a complex family situation. I have also learned a lot about the massive business empire, which has more recently developed around the UK wedding industry.

I would particularly like to thank the following businesses in my hometown of Bexhill for allowing me to use them as part of the setting for this novel.

The Club at the Waterfront
Buenos Aires Guest House
Avra Café Pizza House
That's Amore Café

Claire Baldry

Contents

Part One

Part Two

Part Three

PART ONE

CHAPTER ONE

Monday Lunch

Angie was fastening her jacket when the phone rang. "Mum, it's me. I need a favour."

"Ask quickly then. I've got my jacket on. I was on my way out."

"Why on earth are you wearing a jacket? It's boiling out there." Angie was irritated by her daughter's increasing habit of treating her like a child.

"It's breezy on Bexhill seafront. What do you want, Charlotte? I'm in a hurry."

"Can you pick Joe up from school on Wednesday? His dad's let me down again."

"No, I'm sorry Charlotte, I can't. It's Uncle Jack's funeral on Wednesday."

Angie could hear daughter's annoyance. "I still don't see why you have to go. You didn't like him."

"I'm the only one left now on Grandpa's side. I'm going to represent the family."

"Uncle Jack won't know you're there."

"I'm just doing what I believe is right. Sorry about Joe, but you'll have to find someone else. Charlotte, I have to go." Angie put down the phone. She grabbed her bag and stepped out of her flat and onto the wide landing. She deliberately walked past the lift and descended the four flights of stairs.

"I am not yet old," she told herself, "I have a right to my own life." The July sun was strong. Angie began to feel hot as she hurried along the promenade. She was pleased Charlotte wasn't watching as she removed her jacket. By the time she reached the little Thai restaurant, her friend Alison was already seated at a table. Alison waved an empty glass at Angie.

"Wine? You look flustered."

"I am flustered, and yes please. Well done for remembering to bring the bottle." The restaurant wasn't licensed, so the two friends took it in turns to bring wine to their weekly lunch.

"Let me guess, it's Charlotte."

Angie let out an exaggerated sigh. "She talks down to me as if I'm senile. And she forgets I have a right to a life of my own. I'm her mother, not her servant."

"Drink," instructed Alison.

"Sorry, I shouldn't let her get to me. How are you? How was the doctor's?"

"The blood test showed no signs of cancer, but he's referring me for a scan just as a precaution. He thinks the bloating might be caused by gallstones. I feel much more positive."

"That's brilliant news."

The two women glanced briefly at the menu. This was an unnecessary part of their routine, since they always ordered the same set lunch. As soon as the dishes arrived, the pair absorbed themselves in food and conversation with a closeness which could only be achieved through longstanding friendship. No one, who saw them, could have doubted their intimacy, despite the obvious differences in their choice of fashion and hairstyle. Angie's outfit was tailored and co-ordinated and accompanied by manicured nails and expensively cut and highlighted hair. Alison had the appearance of every item of clothing having been thrown together on the off-chance that the combination might work. Her hands were worn through years of meticulous attention to her garden. Her long heavy locks were whisked away from her face by a large ornate metal clip. Every so often she would remove the clip and pull the grey hair back into submission. They reviewed their week and gossiped extensively about their acquaintances. By the time they parted company, Angie's stress seemed to have disappeared.

CHAPTER TWO

Farewell to Jack

When Angie woke on Wednesday morning, she examined the black dress and grey jacket which were hanging on the front of her wardrobe door. She felt slightly ashamed at feeling so much pleasure in anticipation of wearing the expensive new outfit. The cut of the dress was very forgiving and disguised her middle-aged weight gain. She embarked upon a leisurely late breakfast followed by a bath and hair wash. The family had believed that Robin's father had married beneath himself. They had not been kind to Robin's late mother. Angie had something to prove. Her downstairs neighbour, Stewart, looked up from polishing his car, as Angie walked through the rear parking area towards her garage. She heard him whistle and she smiled. A whistle from a younger man would have been offensive. Stewart, at eighty, was allowed to ignore political correctness.

The journey to the cemetery took less than ten minutes. Angie drove through the elaborate gated entrance and parked in one of the lanes which led to the little chapel. The sun was blazing down from a cloudless sky, and a few mourners were already gathering in the open air. She locked her car and headed towards the chapel. Curious faces turned towards her. Although in her early sixties, Angie's good looks still attracted attention. A younger man, probably in his forties, approached. "Are you family?"

"Jack was my late husband's uncle. I'm his niece by marriage."

"I'm pleased some family are here." He shook Angie's hand. "I was one of Jack's carers at the residential home. He had very few visitors, not that he would have recognised them in his final year."

"I rarely saw Jack, even when he was well. There was some sort of fall-out when my in-laws married, which was never really resolved. Jack's brother was disinherited, and Jack got all his parents' money. I expect they're all together now in heaven bickering. God will probably expel them."

The man grinned. "Jack was very strong-willed. That was one reason why he was allocated male carers. He had no respect for women. Sorry, I shouldn't speak ill of the dead."

"No worries. Do you know anyone else here?" Angie asked.

"The elderly man, Albert, was his neighbour before Jack came to us. He used to visit occasionally. I believe that lady over there was Jack's late wife's niece. I don't know who the others are." The funeral car approached, and an undertaker ushered the small group into the chapel. Angie sat on a wooden pew next to 'the carer'. She must remember to ask his name after the service. Her eyes wandered around the congregation. The pews faced each other so she could examine her fellow mourners without needing to turn her head.

"Who organised the funeral?" Angie whispered to 'the carer'.

"We did the final bit at the care home, but Jack had been well prepared. He purchased a funeral plan and named our solicitor as the executor of his will. It was all tied up before the dementia got too severe." Angie had no time to reply. The sound of bagpipes began to play from a CD player, and the coffin was carried in. Angie had attended several funerals since her husband died ten years earlier. Nevertheless, the sight of a coffin always reawakened her tearful memories of bereavement. She had learned to pinch her hands on such occasions so that the self-inflicted pain distracted her. The skin around her knuckles grew red while she secretly tortured herself. The funeral director spoke. He instructed everyone to sit, before explaining that Jack had requested a non-religious ceremony. A summary of Jack's life was followed by a short silence for reflection. The doors of the chapel then opened, and the coffin was reloaded into the hearse for its final journey to the graveside. The mourners followed on foot. Although filled with tombstones, the hillside provided remarkable breath-taking views towards the sea, a starkly contrasting backdrop to their solemn walk. The coffin was slowly lowered into its resting place, and family were invited to drop handfuls of earth onto the casket. Angie noticed the redness on her hand as she crumbled the soil and watched it tumble through her fingers. After an appropriate silence the mourners returned to their cars. "I don't know your name," she approached the carer.

"I'm Michael."

"Are you coming back to the hotel, Michael?"

"Yes, I'll see you there."

Angie climbed into her car and sat for a moment observing the group. There was the neighbour, Albert, a solitary slightly bent elderly figure, and close by him a much younger, tall lady dressed in a black suit. Michael, the carer, was standing next to two uniformed employees from the undertaker. There was a tall man she didn't recognise, of about her age, with a full head of grey hair, and another couple who she vaguely remembered seeing at her own husband's funeral. She started her car and drove to the hotel.

Even though Angie was the last to arrive, there were plenty of empty spaces in the large car park at the rear of the hotel. She walked past reception and entered a room where the undertaker greeted the guests. Hotel staff were pouring tea and offering neatly-cut sandwiches. Angie tried to steady her teacup whilst attempting to lift a sandwich. "Would you like me to hold your tea?" asked the tall man. "Unless you have three hands, it isn't possible to hold a plate and cup and eat at the same time." He took her cup and placed it on a side table. "I'm Martin, Jack's nephew. One of Miriam's sisters was my aunt."

"You look like Miriam, a male version I mean. Not that I saw her often."

"Good looks run on both sides of the family then." He held her gaze momentarily, and she felt herself blush.

"Have we met before? I don't think I remember you."

Martin grinned. "No. My lot were excommunicated, as I believe your in-laws were. Jack's brother would only speak to Miriam's other sister, my Auntie Florence. Florence married a banker, so she was forgiven."

"Forgiven for what?"

"Well I'm not absolutely sure, but I think a lack of private education was part of my mother's crime. You definitely wouldn't have been accepted. You can't even balance a teacup and a sandwich."

Angie was amused and grateful for Martin's attention. She looked round the room. The tall lady in black was speaking to Albert and Michael, and the other couple were standing on their own.

"Do you know that couple over there?" Angie asked Martin. "I recognise them from my husband's funeral."

Martin quickly glanced down at Angie's wedding ring, then looked at the other couple. "Miriam, Jack's wife, had two sisters, Mary and Florence. Mary was my mother. We were definitely not considered good enough. Rosemary is Florence's daughter. The man is her husband James. Despite their snobbish parents, they're okay. Come on, we'll go and say hello." He placed his hand behind her elbow, and Angie allowed herself to be led towards Rosemary and James.

"I see you've pounced on the only other attractive woman in the room, Martin," grinned James. "How are you, Angela?"

"I'm fine, James, Rosemary." Angie held out her hand to each of them in turn. "I'm sorry, I only just about remember you. You came to Robin's funeral, but I never got the chance to thank you."

"You were hardly in a situation to remember anything at the time. Robin's death was so sudden. I remember that you were very dignified though. We just wanted to represent Jack's side of the family at Robin's funeral. There had been so much bad feeling."

Michael crossed the room to join them. "I have to leave now, Angie, I'm on a late shift."

Angie walked with Michael to the door. "Thank you for looking after Uncle Jack, even if he was difficult."

"Just doing my job," and Michael headed towards his car.

Rosemary and James followed. "We must leave too. It was good to see you again."

"Drive safely." Angie kissed them lightly. She watched Albert and the tall lady walk towards the door and felt guilty at not conversing with them. As the tall lady left she reached out to a plate of sandwiches and discreetly slid them into a plastic bag, before hiding them in her large cloth handbag.

Angie turned towards Martin. "Did you see that?"

"See what?" The tall lady had disappeared.

"It doesn't matter."

Martin hovered. "Can I have your address? I mean you are family. We should do Christmas cards."

Angie felt flustered. She found a business card in her bag and gave it to Martin. "My address is on here. How long is your journey home? I expect your family are missing you."

"I live close by in Eastbourne, and I'm divorced." He took her hand and kissed it with a dramatic flourish. "It's not every day I meet a new cousin. We should do this again." He paused. "I mean meet, not go to a funeral," and Martin was gone.

CHAPTER THREE

Alison's News

When Angie arrived home, an ansaphone message was waiting. It was from Alison. "Angie, it's Alison. I've had some bummer news. The scan showed a problem. Looks like it might be the big C after all. Can you ring me when you've got five minutes?"

Angie poured herself a drink and phoned Alison back. "Tell me everything."

"Well, I didn't really take it all in, but apparently the scan showed a shadow. They did a second blood test after the scan, and that also showed something abnormal. They're taking me in on Monday to do a biopsy."

"D'you want me to come with you?"

"Thank you, sweetie, but no. If you are by my side, I will fall apart. On my own, I will have to be brave. I'll go by taxi, but would appreciate a lift home."

"Of course. Just text me, and I'll come."

"How was the funeral?"

"Quite a small affair, but well organised. Jack had arranged it all before he lost his marbles." Angie paused. "And I met a man, a man who actually paid me some attention, a distant cousin, divorced, lives in Eastbourne."

"Now that has cheered me up. I hope you'll share him. Does he like women without hair, d'you think?" Angie felt shocked at the sudden thought of Alison losing her long hair to chemo.

"I'm sure it won't come to that, Alison. And my meeting with the new man will probably come to nothing as well. He did take my phone number though."

"More and more interesting. Look, I've gotta prepare for Monday. I'll update you by text, when I can."

They ended the call.

A few minutes later Angie's phone bleeped. It was a text from Charlotte.

How was the funeral?

Angie was pleased her daughter had remembered.

Okay, as funerals go. I met some new cousins.

That's random. C U soon.

A second text from Charlotte arrived.

I might have something to tell you x

"Worrying," Angie muttered to herself.

CHAPTER FOUR

Belmont Grange

Belmont Grange was an imposing country house hotel located in the heart of the East Sussex countryside. Built in the eighteenth century as the family home of the Belmont family, it had remained in private ownership until the latter half of the twentieth century. Although well loved by the family, they had struggled to maintain the property in good order. The Belmonts had allowed it to be used as a hospital during the First World War, and to be borrowed by the war office for security purposes during the 1940s. When the late Lord Belmont finally returned to his family home after the Second World War, he soon realised that his inherited income would no longer be enough to maintain the fabric of such a historic building or indeed to employ a sufficiently large team of staff to run the estate. In 1973 he sold his family home to the Magma Consortium who converted the building into a five-star hotel with adjacent golf course.

Magma Consortium went into administration in the 1990s, and the business was split into two parts. The golf course was taken over by a leisure company, whilst the building and a small part of the grounds were purchased by the Sussex multi-millionaire and entrepreneur Kenton Walsh. Now in his sixties, Kenton liked the idea of owning a traditional country house hotel and invested heavily in the project. He uncovered many of the original features which had been hidden behind plasterboard partitions and underneath suspended ceilings. He designed twenty-five individual suites, each named after one of the long list of aristocratic visitors who had stayed with the Belmont family during its four-hundred-year history. The hotel soon became a popular venue for gastronomic breaks and weekend trips to Glyndebourne and Plumpton. When the building was later licensed as a wedding venue, the present manager, Felicity Parks, exploited the growing demand for upmarket and lavish weddings to develop a new, prestigious and profit-making arm of the business. Couples with sufficient budgets were able to take over the entire hotel for the night. Staffing costs were kept as low as possible by using a large bank of trusted casual workers who were employed on zero hours contracts alongside a small permanent team. The role of wedding co-ordinator was created in 1998 shortly after Belmont Grange was granted its licence to conduct ceremonies on the premises. The post was popular and rarely became vacant, but was advertised in the summer of 2018, following the retirement of the previous post-holder. Felicity had decided that she wanted someone who could introduce some fresh new ideas, as well as relating well to both staff and younger guests. A shortlist of three was selected, each applicant being invited to give a short presentation about themselves and their experience, followed by a more formal interview.

When Martin's daughter, thirty-year-old Jessica, saw the advertisement in the *Eastbourne Herald*, she had decided to apply. With a degree in Hotel Management, and having spent several years as a junior manager with a well-known hotel chain in Eastbourne, she felt ready for a promotion. She was delighted when the manager of Belmont Grange phoned to invite her for interview the following Wednesday, the same day that her father attended Jack's funeral.

Jessica felt her heart begin to race as she turned her car into the long gravel drive which led to the hotel. Tall trees shaded the ground, until the roadway curved to reveal the imposing entrance to the hotel. The last blooms of wisteria could still be seen suspended from the twisted branches which surrounded the windows on the lower floors, and an abundance of yellow roses had been trained around the tall arched entrance, softening the grey stonework. She entered the building and was asked to sit and wait in the long entrance hall with two other shortlisted candidates. Jessica glanced nervously at her opposition and smiled. There was a suited man of about her age, clutching a laptop, and a much younger girl who was resting an art portfolio against her legs. Jessica suddenly felt anxious. Eventually, Felicity approached the trio, introduced herself and addressed the candidates. "I realise that my telling you not to be nervous will make no difference, but do try and relax. You will be called for your presentation in reverse alphabetical order, so that means you'll be last, Jessica. There'll be three of us watching you, me, Tina, representing the staff, and Mr Walsh, the owner, who has decided to join us today. Have any of you brought a PowerPoint?"

"I have." The man stood up.

"Well as it happens, Graham, you're first, so I'll take you through to set up."

After Graham had disappeared, the younger girl looked at Jessica. "Were we supposed to bring a PowerPoint?"

"Only if we wanted. I haven't."

"Phew. I thought I'd got it wrong."

Fifteen minutes later the first interviewee reappeared. "I'm sorry we had to cut you a bit short, Graham, but we did specify a ten-minute presentation plus time for questions. We have a lot to get through." She turned towards the young girl. "Your turn now, Lindsay."

The second candidate disappeared, clutching her portfolio.

"How was it?" Jessica asked the man.

"Fine, I think I impressed them. I just ran out of time."

Ten minutes later the younger girl returned.

"Okay?" asked Jessica.

"Sort of. I was very nervous."

"I'm sure you were fine," reassured Jessica.

"Last one then." Felicity had come to fetch Jessica. Jessica picked up her embroidered shoulder bag and followed Felicity into the boardroom. Introductions complete, Jessica placed her bag on the table and pulled out a small toy giraffe. During her own school inset days, Jessica had frequently accompanied her father into work and sat in his classroom. She had observed his skills at captivating an audience. She had watched and learned. She began her presentation.

"This is Cuthbert. He's been my good friend ever since I can remember. He came with me into the operating theatre when, aged six, I had grommets inserted. He comforted me when I was sixteen and my mum and dad split up. He sat on my desk when I completed my final exams for my degree in Hotel Management. He was the first person I told when I got this interview. I find it enormously helpful to know that I have one constant companion to share my stresses and successes."

Jessica glanced at her audience to see if she had caught their attention. Kenton Walsh was smiling, but Felicity was inscrutable. She paused just long enough to ensure they were all paying attention. Jessica then reiterated how families came in all shapes and sizes, how she believed in the importance of strong family relationships and then focussed on marriage. She emphasised how most young couples genuinely believed that their marriage would last forever, and why a wedding day should therefore be very special. She stressed how the couple and their family should be put at the centre of all arrangements. She explained how she didn't believe in pressure selling but knew that building a good relationship with the bride and groom would encourage them to purchase a few extras. After exactly ten minutes, she asked, "Any questions?"

Kenton Walsh grinned. "Just one. Why did you call your giraffe, Cuthbert?"

Jessica giggled. "It was the name of a hippo on children's TV."

"That's logical," Felicity smiled and led Jessica back to the hallway.

There was a wait of about ten minutes, after which Kenton Walsh appeared. He addressed all three candidates. "Firstly, I want to say thank you to all of you for your presentations. You all did very well, and we feel we have learned a lot about you. So we have cut each interview down to about fifteen minutes. Graham, you're first."

Graham reappeared with Felicity promptly after fifteen minutes. Lindsay was next, and her interview seemed to be shorter. There was then a five-minute delay, before Jessica was fetched by Tina. She was invited to sit down in front of the panel. "Jessica, we really enjoyed your entertaining presentation. Is this a skill you learned in your current post?"

"Oh no, I think I learned it from my father. He's a teacher."

Felicity asked, "And if we held the occasional 'bride to be' event, would you be willing to speak?"

"I'd love to."

It was Kenton's turn. "And how flexible can you be about hours, especially at short notice?"

Jessica knew they were not allowed to ask about her family situation.

"I don't have a partner or children, so I can be very flexible." She pulled her hair way from her face, and Kenton found himself wondering why such an attractive, charismatic young woman was apparently unattached. Jessica noticed Felicity and Kenton exchanging glances.

"Okay," started Kenton "One final question, do you want the job?"

"Of course I do. I would love this job."

"Then, if you're happy with the advertised salary, it's yours. When can you start?"

"I suppose, I'd better check about notice with my current work. And thank you so much!"

Felicity stepped in to explain. "Jessica, you were brilliant, exactly what we need at Belmont Grange. We knew as soon as you started your presentation, but of course we had to be fair and interview everyone." She turned to Tina. "Can you go out to Mr 'Death by PowerPoint' and the nervous young girl and tell them that we will write to them and let them know. You'd better stay in here Jessica or they will see you grinning."

Kenton shook Jessica's hand and said he had to go, so she found herself alone with Felicity. "If you have time I will give you a brief tour."

"That would be wonderful."

"I should have done this before the interview," Felicity confessed. "But Kenton turned up unexpectedly and wanted my attention. You'll find he does that from time to time, although just lately he's handed a lot of the responsibility over to his son. I just hope you'll like the place."

"I'm sure I will."

Felicity led Jessica up the wide central staircase to a massive landing. There were doors, each with a separate name plaque, which surrounded the landing. Felicity produced a large bronze key and opened one of them. "This is the Victoria Suite, named because Victoria and Albert stayed here shortly after their marriage. I like to think a young prince might actually have been conceived in this room."

The inner lobby revealed a massive bedroom with four-poster bed and an adjacent and opulently furnished lounge area. "Wow!" gasped Jessica.

"I know, it's amazing, isn't it? I don't think the brochure we sent you does it justice. We tend to use this room as the bridal suite, though all the suites are lovely. Have a look at the bathrooms."

"Bathrooms?"

"Yes, there are two, but only one has a spa bath."

"How primitive," Jessica laughed. She wanted to take a photo, but didn't like to ask. The rest of the tour centred around the public rooms, restaurant, bar area and 'The Orangery', which was licensed for weddings.

"All The Orangery doors open out onto the garden, so in fine weather we can join the indoor and outdoor spaces. We're very flexible about the uses we make of each room, but, of course, we are only allowed to conduct wedding ceremonies in this one room."

Jessica felt quite emotional as she imagined a bride and groom standing in front of the long oak table. "It's a big responsibility to get it right."

"I have every faith in you, and you'll have a good team to back you up." Felicity walked Jessica out through another door. They passed along a corridor until they were back in the boardroom. Jessica picked up her bag, and Felicity handed her the toy giraffe. "Don't forget Cuthbert."

"Thank you. I feel really excited now. I'll talk to work tomorrow, then give you a ring if that's okay?"

"Perfect."

Felicity walked Jessica to her car. "Drive carefully, you've had a hard day."

CHAPTER FIVE

Jessica's News

Martin lived alone in a small terraced house near to Eastbourne town centre. The front garden was paved with room for one small car. He drove back from Jack's funeral and reversed his Fiat into the drive. He had been forced to sell the larger family home and his expensive car twelve years ago in order to pay for his share of the divorce settlement. He had since scraped together enough money to buy his current house and had recently retired from his role as Head of English at Eastbourne High. His ex-wife had her own retirement income, so Martin had been allowed to keep both his pension and the voluntary redundancy payment. He was not especially well-off, but suspected he had more funds than many divorcees. He had intended to purchase a larger car, but the Fiat fitted easily into the drive, and he had grown fond of it.

Martin inserted the key into the front door lock and let himself in. He walked around the ground floor and found himself examining each room with a renewed perspective. The furniture was functional, but second-hand. The kitchen units needed replacing. The carpets had been there when he moved in. They were patterned and faded. His weekly housekeeper ensured that the house was reasonably clean, and he was a tidy person, but could he really bring a woman to visit? He thought about Angie in her expensive black dress with tailored jacket. Her hair had been beautifully cut, and he had noticed a faint aroma of designer perfume. A widow was likely to have benefitted from substantial life insurance. Would she be interested in a man who lived in a tiny terraced house in a back-road in Eastbourne? "You could be punching well above your weight, Martin," he told himself. He considered ringing James and asking about Angie, but didn't want to reveal his interest. Instead he took her card from his suit pocket and read it again. It was a plain understated business card, with the words 'Interior Design Consultant' and then just a name, address and contact details. He turned on his laptop and Googled her address. It threw up a prestigious block of flats on Bexhill seafront. He went onto Zoopla and checked out the prices. They were definitely 'high-end'. He regretted not noticing what car she was driving. He then searched for her name... Angela Stewart, Bexhill. The search threw up over fifty names, and he gave up.

Martin poured himself a beer and reluctantly decided to sleep on his decision. He realised that if Angie was interested, and he had noticed her blush, she would be disappointed that he hadn't called her straight away. He didn't want to play games with her feelings, but he was nervous. His thoughts were interrupted by the phone. "Dad, how are you? How was the funeral?"

"It was okay. Your Auntie Rosemary was there with James, looking as upmarket as ever. How are you? Have you got any news?"

"I have, Dad. I've got the job. I am now the official wedding co-ordinator for the Belmont Grange Hotel. I'm hoping that Channel View will waive some of my notice, and I can start in the next week or so."

"That is such good news. I'm really proud of you. Will I get to look round?"

"I hope so Dad. It's an amazing place. I even get a discount on my own wedding, if ever I plan one, but it is grossly expensive."

Martin was pleased that he had managed to retain a good relationship with his daughter after the divorce. "What did Mum say? Was she pleased?"

"I haven't told her yet. She's in Prague with work. I'll text her later."

Martin felt a guilty pleasure at being the first parent to be told. "Why don't you come round, if you're not busy? Bring a takeaway. I'll pay. We can celebrate."

"Okay, Dad. I'll bring the hotel brochures to show you. Might stay over if you don't mind. Then I can have a drink." Aware that his daughter's presence overnight might further delay his phone call to Angie, Martin reluctantly agreed.

An hour later, Jessica arrived with a large Chinese takeaway, two bottles of wine, a handful of hotel brochures and a bill for her father. Once filled with stir fry and Chardonnay, father and daughter browsed through the glossy hotel brochures. "It will be my job to co-ordinate the weddings. It's a big responsibility." Jessica looked up at her father. "Don't you get fed up with living on your own?" she asked unexpectedly.

"Yes, I do," he replied. "But I don't miss the constant rowing with your mother."

"You know she's got a bloke... a boyfriend," Jessica exaggerated the word 'boyfriend'.

"I guessed," Martin replied. "She's taking a lot more trouble over her appearance these days. Do you mind?"

"It's fine, Dad. I quite like him." Martin felt a pang of jealousy. "I'm surprised you haven't found someone else too. I mean someone a bit more permanent. You've got loads more hair than most men of your age, and you seem pretty fit." The alcohol filled them both with confidence.

"Actually, Jess, I met someone yesterday, at the funeral, a distant cousin. Thought I might give her a ring."

"You should."

Martin hesitated. "I'm just a bit worried."

"About me? I really don't mind, Dad."

"That's kind, Jess, but I have other concerns."

"What's wrong with her?"

He grinned. "There's nothing wrong with her, but I think she has money. I'm not sure that she'll approve of my little car and tatty home."

It turned into one of those moments when the offspring suddenly exhibit more maturity than the parent. "If she likes you enough, she won't care about your finances. Have you arranged to see her again?"

"She gave me her phone number. I said I'd ring."

"Do it now, Dad."

"Not while you're here."

"Tomorrow then. Promise me."

"I promise I'll think about it." It had been a tiring day for both of them. They closed the conversation and turned in for the night.

At 7.30 am the phone rang. "Martin? It's Penny from Eastbourne Primary. Can you do a day's supply?"

Martin yawned. "Probably yes, what class?"

"That's the problem. It's reception."

"You know I don't normally do reception. I'm secondary trained, for God's sake."

"We're desperate. Two staff off on a course, and now one more down with flu. I've made five phone calls already, and the little ones do love you."

"Oh, all right then, but I won't be early. Carol will have to prep the room."

"You're a star, Martin. I'll order you a lunch."

"I'll be with you as soon as I can."

Martin put down the phone and hurried upstairs. Jessica was on the landing in her dressing gown.

"Problem?"

"I've got a day's supply. Daren't turn it down, or they won't phone again. I need the money. It's reception infants."

"Poor kids."

"Actually, they love me. Help yourself to breakfast and remember to drop the latch when you leave. Sorry to rush."

"Just get on, Dad, I'll be fine. I'm on a late shift today."

Martin dressed, shaved quickly and grabbed his briefcase. He was in his car by 8.15 am and, despite the traffic, arrived at school in time to receive the children. Carol greeted the parents in the cloakroom, making a note of any overnight concerns before sending the children into the classroom. Their young faces lit up, as they burst through the door. "Mr Black, you came back to us! Have you brought the dragon book to read again?"

"I have, Maisie. The dragon missed you all so much, I had to bring him back." Martin removed the large dragon book from his bag and placed it on the armchair in the carpet area. The National Curriculum would slip a bit in his care, but he knew how to bring a book to life. With Carol's help, he was sure he would survive the day.

Martin arrived home at 5 pm after his day's supply. He had completed the individual children's records while Carol prepared the room for the next day. Penny had popped in to thank him and see if he would be free to teach a year five class the following week, if needed. "I can't do Monday," he had lied, "but I could manage the rest of the week." He parked his car on the front hard-standing and walked through the nearby alleyway to the rear of his house. Jessica had remembered to secure the door, and Martin fumbled through his bag for the key. He peered through the kitchen window and noticed the loaded dishwasher and a handwritten note on the worktop. He unlocked the door and picked up the note.

Thank you for a lovely evening. Make sure you ring your cousin. I expect a report xxx

Martin ran the tap and rinsed the sand and glitter from his hands. He filled the kettle and walked into his small living room, placing Angie's card beside the phone. He sank into a chair. His legs ached from kneeling beside small tables.

Teaching young children should be restricted to adults whose bodies bend more easily, he reflected.

He picked up the card and turned it over in his fingers.

I'll ring her tomorrow.

CHAPTER SIX

The Phone Call

Angie's phone rang at exactly 9.45 am on Friday morning. Martin had decided to time the call for after breakfast, but hopefully before Angie went out. She answered straight away. "Hello?"

"Hi, Angie, it's Martin, your many times removed cousin, remember?"

Angie found herself blushing. She was expecting a call from Charlotte. "Of course I remember."

"I would have rung yesterday, but I had to work."

"I thought you were retired."

"I am mostly, but I take the occasional supply day, well whenever I can fit it in really."

"Eastbourne High?"

"No, reception class at Eastbourne Primary."

Angie laughed. "You're joking! I thought you were a secondary English teacher."

"I was, but I do mostly older primary these days. They tempted me with a load of Duplo and an outdoor sand pit. I've still got sand in my shoes." Martin paused. "So you see, I am in need of grown-up company. Are you busy on Sunday?"

Angie felt flushed. "Not especially."

"Maybe lunch then?"

"That sounds nice."

"Shall I pick you up? I thought we could go to The Peacock, just outside Battle. It's very good."

"Okay." Angie suddenly grew nervous. "What time?"

"12.15?"

"Right then, I'll wait outside the front. You can't miss the flats. They dominate the far end of West Parade. You've got the address, haven't you?"

"I have. Oh, Angie, just one more thing, you won't mind slumming it in my small Fiat?"

Angie laughed, "Of course not... I mean it's not slumming it. It'll be great to be driven by someone else."

"See you on Sunday, then."

"Yes, Sunday," Angie ended the call. She was surprised to find her hand shaking as she replaced the handset. She slowly stood up and walked towards the long mirror in the hallway. There was enough space for her to step back and examine the entire length of her body. She wished she hadn't put on so much weight recently.

The phone rang again, and Angie jumped. She lifted the handset in the hall and spoke nervously.

"Hello?"

"Angie, it's Alison. Are you okay? You sound a bit strange."

"I'm fine, just in shock. More to the point, how are you?"

"Okay, as ever, well a bit twitchy about Monday, but nothing you wouldn't expect. What d'you mean in shock? Is it Charlotte?"

"No, for once it's not Charlotte, I've got a date... at least I think it's a date."

"With him? The cousin?"

"Sunday lunch... that's the day after tomorrow."

"Oh yes, I need a distraction. Tell me more."

"We're going to The Peacock. He's picking me up. I don't know what to wear. I feel fat."

"Stuff and nonsense, most women would pay a fortune for your figure, women of your age anyway."

"Thanks… I think."

"You know what I mean. You're lovely. He obviously thinks that anyway. D'you want to go shopping? Can I come? I need a distraction. What about Eastbourne?"

"Yes to the shopping, no to Eastbourne. He lives in Eastbourne, and we might be spotted. Are you sure you have the energy for shopping?"

"Angie, I feel fine, apart from shitting myself with fear. If the consultant hadn't been so doom and gloom about the cancer, I wouldn't even have known I was ill. I'm trying to forget about it until Monday. Let's go to Hastings by train tomorrow, have lunch, drink wine, buy clothes."

Angie set aside her desire to shop alone. Alison needed her.

"11.15 train? Meet at the station?"

"Perfect."

CHAPTER SEVEN

Saturday Lunch

Shopping trips in Hastings were yet another well-rehearsed routine for the two women. The following day, they found themselves walking from Hastings Station to the centre of town for their customary retail route before deciding on a lunch venue. "So you're absolutely sure? The light blue top with trousers?"

"Yes. The colour suits me, and it covers my lumpy middle."

"But is it posh enough? You are going out for lunch."

"I don't want to frighten him away and I don't think he's too flush for money. He still does supply teaching. I can posh it up with a scarf or a necklace."

"Have you got any suitable accessories?"

"I have drawers full. Enough to start my own shop." Angie paused. "Alison, do you mind if I pop back and pay for the top now? I don't want them to sell it."

"Go on then, but don't be long or I'll drink your wine."

"Don't you dare. I'll be ten minutes maximum. I mustn't change my mind again."

True to her word, Angie returned to the little Italian restaurant just as the olives and bread were being delivered to the table. She sat back down and took a bite of bread. "I just feel a fraud, all churned up like this. I'm not a teenager. I'm being ridiculous."

"It's lovely to see my calm sensible friend in such a state. You deserve this, Angie. It's been ten years now since Robin died, and, let's face it, he wasn't always easy. Sorry, am I allowed to say that?"

"Martin might not be easy. He might be bad-tempered and obnoxiously right-wing, like Uncle Jack."

"He was a teacher in a state school, he's hardly likely to be right-wing. And didn't you say he did supply with reception infants? That sounds a pretty placid thing to do. Don't they cook a lot with the children, reception teachers? You'll be wearing matching aprons and making scones together in no time at all. He can steady your hand as you count out the cups full of flour."

The waiter listened to the women giggle at the scene which Alison had created, while he placed two large bowls of pasta on the table. "This won't help the lumpy waist."

"Fear not, you will worry it off with nerves in the morning."

CHAPTER EIGHT

Sunday Lunch

Angie had planned her Sunday morning... a slow start, breakfast, bath, hair wash, phone excuses ready in case Charlotte rang. Her schedule worked well, until the doorbell rang while she was washing her hair. She wrapped her soapy head in a towel and opened the door wearing her dressing gown. It was Frank, her new neighbour. He had only moved in two weeks ago, and Angie was already tired of his intrusions. This was the fifth visit. "I was wondering if you heard a strange noise last night? There was a lot of banging on the stairs. I thought maybe someone had broken in."

"I doubt it, Frank. The flats are very secure. If you are worried, report it to the committee."

"Oh I will. In fact, I was thinking of standing for election to the committee. They could do with someone from my military background."

"I'm sure they would appreciate your input, Frank. Now if you don't mind, I'm getting ready to go out for lunch."

"Anywhere nice?"

"Just somewhere local."

"I could do with a recommendation of somewhere local for Sunday lunch." Angie began to close the door and manoeuvre Frank onto the landing.

"Well, I'll come back at a more convenient time, shall I?"

"Please do," retorted Angie firmly as she shut the door in his face. "For God's sake!" she muttered, as she returned to the shower to rinse the soap from her hair.

Despite the setback, by midday Angie was dressed in the suitably accessorised blue top and trousers and giving herself a final examination in the hall mirror. She picked up her handbag from the living room and noticed a red Fiat below, parked on the roadside at the front of the flats. "Time to go."

She took a deep breath and headed for the lift. Thankfully Frank was nowhere to be seen.

It was a calm July day. Martin watched Angie emerge round the corner from the back of the flats. He stepped out of the car and opened the passenger door. "You look nice."

"Thank you, and so do you."

"I've booked a table for 1 pm so we have plenty of time. Have you been there before?"

"A couple of times, with Robin and Charlotte." Martin felt unreasonably disappointed. "It was always very good," Angie added. "I've been looking forward to it." There was a silence in the car, which Angie felt obliged to fill. "Have you lived in Eastbourne long?"

"I moved there after I split with Karen. I was still Head of English at Eastbourne High, so it was convenient. We lived in Seaford before that. What about you? Didn't you and Robin live in Croydon?"

"When we first married, yes. Robin managed a betting shop in the town centre. Of course, Jack didn't approve. Even when Robin was promoted, Jack was very negative towards his nephew, said it was a waste of a private education. That's when the rows really started. We moved to Bexhill just after Charlotte was born. By then Robin was area manager and could live anywhere in the South East. A lot of people in Bexhill used to live in Croydon."

Martin grinned. "A whole town full of refugees from Croydon. No wonder it's such an odd place!"

"It is a bit quirky, but I've learnt to love it."

Martin was worried he might have offended Angie and changed the subject. "How old is Charlotte now?"

"She's twenty-four. She was fourteen when Robin died. She was extremely fond of her father and took his death very badly. We've travelled a hard road together." Martin decided not to ask Angie to explain. He was relieved when he turned the Fiat into the pub car park, and they could escape from the confined space of his small car.

The Peacock was busy. A member of staff directed them to a table. "Thank goodness I booked. Drink?" asked Martin.

"White wine, please. Pinot if they have it."

Martin headed for the bar and returned with a large glass of white wine and a pint of shandy. He handed a menu to Angie. "We have to order at the bar. There's a carvery or other options. D'you want a starter?"

"I'm not used to eating large meals at lunchtime. Do you?" Angie didn't want to tell Martin she was watching her weight.

"I'd be happy with just a carvery, but don't let me stop you."

"Just a carvery is fine." They were not easy with each other, and sorting out their menu choices seemed unnecessarily clumsy. Angie took a large mouthful of wine. Martin returned to the bar and returned with two carvery vouchers. "The system's changed since I was last here, but it looks very nice."

Queueing for the food and watching the slices of meat carved and placed on their plates, provided a welcome break from conversation. They were soon seated, large plates of food before them, and Angie began to feel more relaxed. Her wine glass was half-empty, and Martin responded to her change of mood. "Do you do this often?"

"Do what?"

"Eat lunch with distant cousins?"

Angie grinned. "Not often enough." She dared to be flirtatious.

"There must be loads of us," continued Martin. "You could take up genealogy and search for lunch companions."

"I don't think my blood pressure would cope."

"Is lunch with me that stressful?"

"Not at all," she lied. "I just don't feel I know you very well."

"Well, hopefully, we can begin to put that right."

The ice was broken, and Angie wondered if Martin had noticed her blush. He left his food and brought her another glass of wine. The conversation began to flow. Martin described his day in the Eastbourne reception class and entertained Angie with descriptions of his attempts to build sandcastles and tie shoelaces. Angie talked about how she had set up her business as a home design consultant, and why she still retained a few of the more affluent clients. "I bet your flat is full of useless items, just because they look beautiful," guessed Martin, "the opposite of a man-cave."

"Actually, I think most people think my flat is slightly eccentric. Robin tended to treat our house like a showroom. Now I can do what I like, I like to experiment with design. The flat itself is very plain so it needs a bit of imagination."

Martin wanted to say he'd like to see it, but thought that might sound rather forward. "What made you move there?"

"It's convenient, and secure, and someone else deals with the maintenance. Once Charlotte left home, I really didn't need to be rattling around in our old house. Moving was a sensible decision, though the neighbours can be a bit intrusive. Each block has a committee, and it causes stupid quarrels sometimes. I try to keep out of it."

When the meal was over, Martin and Angie returned to his car as more than acquaintances, though each wondered how far their relationship had really progressed. On the journey home, Angie told Martin about Alison.

CHAPTER NINE

Hospital

Alison texted Angie at 2 pm.

Be ready in 30 mins.

On my way.

Angie wanted to ask if Alison was okay, but was fearful of the answer. She grabbed her bag and hurried to her car. The drive to the hospital took twenty minutes. Alison was dressed and sitting in the day room waiting. "Ready to go?"

"Yes."

Angie waited until they were approaching the car park before asking, "Well?"

"Well what?"

"How was it? What did they find?"

"It's a bloody great tumour. In my stomach. They've not got the results of the biopsy, but they know it's cancer. Already spread to my liver."

"Can they remove it?"

"They're going to try. I'm booked in for Wednesday."

"They're not wasting time then."

They got into the car. "Do you want to come back to mine?"

"No, thank you. I want to go home. Get my head together. How did it go? With the Sunday lunch cousin?"

"Good. I think. Once we got over our awkwardness."

"Why, only 'I think'?"

"I'm not sure if he liked me."

"How could he not like you?"

"He didn't touch me. I mean not even a handshake."

"Perhaps he was shy."

"He wasn't shy."

"Nervous then."

"Maybe."

"Has he arranged to see you again?"

"No."

"You think he will?"

"I'm having doubts now."

"His loss, if he doesn't." Angie parked the car outside Alison's house. "I might die, you know. I asked them. They said my chances are about fifty/fifty. I'm pleased I don't have children. I wouldn't want to have to tell them."

"You're a fighter, Alison. You can beat this."

"I'm not sure I want to."

"You're tired. Things will look different tomorrow."

"I'm sure they will. Please don't come in. I need some solitude."

Angie watched her friend enter her house, then drove to the flat. She parked her car in the garage and took the lift to the fourth floor. Frank was hovering outside her door. "Can I have a word?"

"Not now, Frank. Now is not a good time." Angie unlocked the door and entered her flat, leaving Frank on the landing. She walked straight into her kitchen and discovered unstoppable tears rolling down her cheeks. Her phone vibrated with a text.

How was your friend?

She checked the number. The text was from Martin. She waited a few minutes to let the tears subside, then added Martin's number to her contacts.

Going back on Weds for surgery and chemo. Not looking good.

The landline rang. "It's Martin. I thought you might appreciate a friendly voice. Tell me to go away if my call is not welcome."

"Martin, thank you," Angie blinked back the tears. "It's good of you to ring, thoughtful."

"It's not healthy to bottle things up on your own. Tell me about your friend."

And Angie found herself explaining to Martin about Alison's tumour, the chemo, and what the hospital had said. "She was very down when I left her. I don't think I was much help."

"Of course you helped. You were there, weren't you? Alison will need time to process what's happened. Are you going with her on Wednesday?"

"I don't know. I didn't ask her."

"Maybe you should."

"I will. Martin, it's very kind of you to phone. I don't feel I should burden you with all this emotional stuff."

"You need to talk, and I'm a good listener. Not all men are emotionally inept, you know."

Angie felt slightly disconcerted. She had spent her entire married life with a man who kept his own and his wife's emotions at a distance. She had believed all men were like Robin. She found herself wondering if Martin might be gay. "I don't want to intrude, Angie, but I hope we can meet again soon."

"Yes, of course." Her head was swimming. "I'm just a bit all over the place this evening."

"Is that your way of letting me down gently?"

"No, not at all. I want to see you again." There was a pause. "Look, I'll ring you, later, when I've spoken to Alison and got my head back together." Angie needed to think.

"That's a plan then." Martin ended the call. He returned the handset to its housing and spoke out loud. "I think you've just blown it, Martin."

Angie phoned Alison. "Just checking you're okay. Well not okay, but you know what I mean."

"I have dosed myself with alcohol."

"Is that allowed?"

"I didn't ask."

"D'you want a lift on Wednesday?"

"I have to be there early. It would be a 7 am pick-up."

"I need to feel I'm doing something."

"Then, yes please, I would like a lift. Apparently, I will be out of it for most of the day, so once they've taken me down for the chop, you won't be needed."

"I'll collect you at seven then. You'll be doing me a favour. I need to focus on something which isn't a man."

"He didn't ring then."

"Oh yes, he rang, and texted, and he wants to see me again, and he was very lovely, not at all like most men I know, and I feel very confused. I'm worried he may not be as nice as he seems."

"You have got it bad, haven't you? What's your worry?"

"Well, this might sound stupid, but I'm not used to a man who seems to care about my emotional well-being. D'you think he's normal?"

Alison laughed out loud. "For an intelligent woman, you say some really stupid things sometimes. Next thing you'll tell me is you're worried he's gay."

Angie remained silent, so Alison continued, "Look, sweetie, I may not have been successful in maintaining a long-term relationship, but I have worked my way through a lot of men. They are all different and they are all a mystery. I know that's what they say about us, but it works both ways. You can't compare an emotionally empty manager of a chain of betting shops with an apparently sensitive English teacher who is happy to spend a day with a class of five-year-olds. You might just have struck lucky. Do you know why his first marriage broke up?"

"I didn't like to ask."

"Well maybe you should. I bet he had an affair. These sensitive types need a lot of loving."

"Oh, Alison, you do make me smile."

"And you have taken my mind off my own troubles. Go ring him, and I expect a full report in the car on Wednesday. Now I'm going to bed. I suddenly feel very tired."

"Night, Alison, and thank you."

"You're very welcome."

Angie picked up her mobile. What if he had had an affair? Would she mind? At least it would prove he wasn't gay. She suddenly realised how sheltered her life with Robin had been. She wouldn't want to have been like Alison, but maybe a bit more 'man' experience would have been useful. Martin might want to have sex with her. Would she want it? He would need to see her naked. Would she be good enough for him? She poured herself a drink and composed a text.

Is now a convenient time to ring?

Yes x

Crikey he put a kiss. Was that relevant, she wondered?

She picked up the landline and dialled his number.

"I'm pleased you phoned. Is your friend okay?"

"Yes, well sort of. She made me laugh. I'm taking her to the Conquest Hospital on Wednesday."

"Good. If you can be of use to her, it'll make you feel better." He hesitated. "So when can we meet? I might be working next week, so how about Saturday?"

"Saturday's good."

"Where would you like to go?"

"I don't know," said Angie. "It depends on the weather, I s'pose. I'll drive if you like."

Martin became more upbeat. "Let's do something frivolous, like a boating lake or a zoo. You need to lift your spirits. I'll try and think of somewhere we can go by train, then neither of us will need to drive."

"That sounds fun. Maybe we can decide on Thursday or Friday after watching the weather forecast?"

"Perfect," agreed Martin. "I'll ring you Thursday evening."

"Martin, before you hang up, can I ask you something?"

"That sounds worrying. Yes, of course you can."

"Why did your marriage break up?"

"You don't know? I thought you would have heard. Families do like to gossip."

"No, I don't know."

"Oh dear," groaned Martin, "this might blow it then." He took a deep breath. "I had an affair, well not really an affair, a one-night stand, with the head of RE at my school. We got drunk together on a residential leadership course. I felt so guilty afterwards that I went home and confessed. I stupidly thought Karen would forgive me, but she slung me out. It was a proper soap opera moment, suitcases on the pavement and locks changed. I had to sofa surf for several weeks before I could find somewhere to rent. To be honest, I think she was looking for an excuse to get rid of me. I later discovered there was another man waiting in the wings, though that's not the one she's with now."

Angie was silent. "Speak to me, Angie. I need to know what you're thinking." Martin couldn't stop talking. "I wouldn't do that to you. I wouldn't have the energy to sleep with more than one woman at my age. Sorry that was a really stupid thing to say. You shouldn't sleep with more than one person at any age. Of course, you might not want to sleep with me, but if you do, eventually, I wouldn't let you down, I really wouldn't. God I've really blown it now, haven't I?"

"Martin, maybe you should stop talking and listen for a minute. You said you were good at listening."

"I am listening."

"You haven't blown it. I just wanted to know. As for the other stuff, I might possibly want to sleep with you at some point in the future, but I think we should get to know each other a bit better before we consider it."

Martin laughed. "So I don't completely repulse you then?"

"You're a very attractive, and moderately sane man."

"That is the nicest thing anyone has said to me for a long time."

"So maybe you should go now, before you really do blow it."

"Yes, cousin. I will ring you on Thursday."

Angie ended the call. On impulse she picked up her mobile and sent Martin a text.

Goodnight Cousin x

Sweet Dreams xx came the instant reply.

It was too late to turn back now, but she did wonder what she had got herself into.

CHAPTER TEN

Second Date

Martin rang Angie on Thursday evening. "Hello, cousin, are you still talking to me?"

"I am." Angie was pleased that Martin had rung.

"Any news about Alison?"

"I visited her today. She was wired up to God knows what, and a bit drowsy, but she spoke a few words. Her sister is coming down for a week, so I won't need to visit every day. How are you? Did you work today?"

"Yesterday and today, year five. That's a nice age, pre-adolescent, but at least they can tie their own shoelaces. And the tables are taller. I don't get so much backache. I'm off tomorrow, saving my energy for you. Have you thought where we could go?"

"Nope, but I bet you have."

Martin smiled to himself. "I have given it some thought. We could do something educated, but you might show me up, so why don't we go to the caves in Hastings. We could take the West Hill Lift and do the Smugglers Adventure. Maybe have a late lunch in the Old Town? The forecast is good so we can walk to Hastings Old Town from the station. D'you like fish?"

"That sounds great, really. And I love fish. I've been meaning to check out the Smugglers Adventure to see if Joe would like it."

"Who's Joe?"

"Charlotte's son. He's six. Charlotte fell pregnant when she was eighteen, and refused to marry the dad, though they still share care of Joe. Robin would have been mortified."

"You are full of surprises. If I look out for you at Bexhill station we could catch the same train. Can you make the 11.15? It only has two carriages, so we shouldn't miss each other. I'll be in the front carriage. Any problems, we can text."

"Quarter past eleven, Bexhill station, this Saturday, a two-carriage train, front carriage, I can do that. So you don't need to ring me tomorrow."

"Don't you want me to ring you?"

"It might be easier if you didn't. Charlotte said she might come over."

Martin didn't argue.

A text for Angie arrived on Saturday morning.

Trains all on time so far x

Thank you for letting me know x

How was Charlotte? X

She didn't come. Gotta go. Need time to get ready x

Okay see you later xx

Angie arrived at Bexhill station in plenty of time. She stood on platform two and waited for the train. She wished her stomach would stop churning. The train arrived, and Martin was standing in the open doorway of the front carriage. He stretched out his arm to help her onto the train. They sat next to each other. He took her hand and twisted her fingers between his. She was surprised at how her body responded to his touch. "Who are those two girls looking at us?" asked Martin.

"Could be friends of Charlotte. I doubt they know who I am." They alighted in Hastings and walked out of the station, past the medical centre towards the seafront.

Martin took Angie's hand as soon as the crowds allowed. "All right?"

"Yes," she smiled, "I feel like an escaping teenager."

"You look like a beautiful woman."

"Martin, you don't have to flatter me."

"I'm not flattering you. You are very beautiful. I'm proud to be with you." She briefly wondered if those were the words he used to lure the head of RE, but tried to set aside that thought.

"Don't overthink everything," Alison had advised. "Just enjoy it. Enjoy being with him."

Angie gave Martin's hand a squeeze. As they drew closer to Hastings Old Town, they could see the lift ascending West Cliff.

"It looks a bit geriatric," observed Angie. "Have you been on it before?"

"It's Victorian, so has been carrying passengers forever. No, I've not been on it, but I really want to." Having insisted on paying her way, Angie took her ticket and stepped into the small carriage. She felt a flutter of excitement as the glass-fronted funicular railway ascended the cliff side.

"All right?"

"I love it."

Martin relaxed. He helped her out of the lift, and they climbed the narrow steps which led out to West Hill. Martin put his arm around her. He was a lot taller than Angie so his arm rested easily across her shoulders. "It's this way."

The sky was cloudless, and the sea was a Mediterranean green. As they stared towards the horizon, they could see a heat haze building up above the water. "It's stunning, like being on a Greek island!" exclaimed Angie. Once inside the caves, Martin took Angie's hand. The light was dim, and smugglers and pirates appeared unexpectedly, acting out their story. The actors took every opportunity to make the adults and older children jump.

"Are you okay?" whispered Martin.

"It's great."

When they finally emerged from the caves, they stopped momentarily, so their eyes could adjust to the light. "I've booked a table at Macks for 1.30, so we can take our time getting back down in the lift." Martin held Angie's hand, as they walked back to the lift.

This is a man who likes women, she thought. *He likes to look after women. He enjoys the company of women, but am I just a conquest?* She wished she felt more secure.

Macks was a speciality fish restaurant on Hastings seafront. Angie had always wanted to try it. She was delighted when the waiter showed them to a seat on the covered veranda which overlooked the tall wooden net huts. They read the menu. "I can't afford to eat at places like this too often," Martin confessed, "but I wanted us to have a special day." It was as if he was reading Angie's thoughts. "I'm not doing this to try and seduce you, Angie. There's no payback... even though you won't let me pay for you. I just like you, I like you a lot and I wanted us to enjoy ourselves." If Martin had been trying to seduce her, he would have sensed the promise of success. She was falling under his spell. There followed shared plates of mussels and crab and seared scallops with langoustine ready to dip into garlic butter. They forked up the delicacies and passed them to each other between sips of dry white wine. Martin spooned up the garlic butter. "It's a good thing we're sharing this. I wouldn't be able to get near you otherwise." He leant across the table and kissed her on the cheek. "I hope that wasn't too full of garlic." Yet again, Angie blushed.

They paid, half each, and slowly walked back to the station, hand in hand. "You got your ticket?"

"Yes, teacher."

"Sorry, I can't help organising people," Martin apologised. "Will you be okay walking back on your own? I could walk you back if you like, but I have to see Jessica this evening. She starts her new job soon, and I promised her yet another takeaway. Not that I'll eat much. She can take the leftovers home."

"I'll be fine. I'm a big girl, and it's not dark. You stay on the train to Eastbourne." Angie alighted at Bexhill with mixed emotions. She was disappointed that Martin had not offered to come back to her flat. She wanted to show him her home. She wanted him to take her in his arms. She knew she would have made love to him. In many ways she felt ready. However, although Martin had shown affection on their day out, he had barely kissed her. Her sensible side said it was too early for sex. She might have doubted his motives. Emotionally, she needed to take more time, but her body had other ideas. She was aching for him.

Back at the flat, her ansaphone was flashing. She briefly wondered if it might be Martin, but reminded herself he would still be on his way home. It was Charlotte. "Mum, I need to see you. Ollie and I have something to tell you. Can we come for coffee tomorrow morning?"

Charlotte sounded anxious, and Angie spoke her thoughts out loud. "Please don't let Charlotte be pregnant."

Angie phoned back. "Hi Charlotte, good to hear from you. Is everything okay?"

"Yes, fine. Sorry, I've not been in touch, I've been busy. I've got some good news, but Ollie says we must tell you in person, so you'll have to wait until tomorrow. We'll be round about eleven-ish. Is that okay?"

"Fine. I'll look forward to it. D'you want to stay for lunch?"

"No, we'll be far too busy. Got things to do." There was a silence, then Charlotte spoke again. "You were spotted, you know…"

"Spotted?"

"Today on the train, holding hands with a man. Aren't you a bit old for that sort of thing?"

Angie was taken by surprise. "And what sort of thing would that be, Charlotte?"

"You know… men."

"You think I'm too old for everything."

"No, I don't, Mum, but people do expect senior citizens to show a bit of dignity."

"Don't lecture me, Charlotte, you're less than half my age."

"Well someone has to. Anyway, you'll be far too busy to do anything stupid, once you hear our news. I can't wait to tell you."

"Will Joe be with you?"

"No, it's his dad's weekend, but I'll need you to have him a lot in the next few weeks. I'll have lots to do."

Angie took a deep breath. "I'll check my diary when you come."

The phone rang again. It was Martin. "Just checking you got home safely."

"Yes, I managed a whole ten-minute walk, unaccompanied." She sounded prickly.

"Sorry, I didn't mean to be over-protective. Is everything all right?"

"I've had Charlotte on the phone. We were spotted holding hands on the train. She gave me a lecture about dignified behaviour."

"How old is she?"

"Twenty-four."

"Not a stage in life known for its knowledge about dignified behaviour. Jess was all over the place at that age. I'm sorry if I've caused you embarrassment."

"You haven't. I'm just annoyed with Charlotte. She thinks I have no right to a life of my own. She probably thinks sex stops at forty."

"Doesn't it? Anyway, we haven't had sex. At least, not in real life. I have in my head though, with you, I can't seem to help myself."

"Martin, you're embarrassing me."

"Good. That was the intention, to take your mind off Charlotte. She'll come round, once she experiences the Martin Black charm."

"She can be tricky, Martin."

"She's twenty-four. We'll deal with her."

Angie liked the 'we'. "Anyway, apparently, they have something important to tell me. They're coming round tomorrow morning. I hope to God she isn't pregnant again."

"I won't ring you tomorrow then. No point in inflaming the situation. Get back to me when you can." Martin added, "Angie, I did enjoy today. I hope you did too."

"It was special."

"It was, wasn't it. Good luck tomorrow." He ended the call.

Angie felt flustered. She tried to focus on what Charlotte's news would be, but her thoughts kept drifting towards Martin. Was he really fantasising about having sex with her? Was it just physical sex in his mind, or was he looking for a long-term relationship? She realised she wanted both. She imagined him making love to her with long and lingering passion. She couldn't shake off the image. If only she could ring Alison for advice.

CHAPTER ELEVEN

Charlotte's News

The following day Angie buzzed Ollie and Charlotte into the building at half-past ten. They used the stairs and were soon knocking on the flat door. "I've got the kettle on. I thought you might be early."

Angie carried a tray of mugs into the living room. Despite a slight sea breeze, the weather was sultry, and she had opened the balcony doors.

Ollie admired the view. "The sea really does look spectacular from up here. No wonder these flats sell at a premium. I was looking at the prices on Rightmove."

"Are you house-hunting, Ollie? I thought you and Charlotte were happy at your place." Ollie was older than Charlotte, and Angie found him easy to talk to.

"We are happy, but we've been thinking about the future. I'll let Charlotte explain."

Charlotte held out her left hand. "You haven't noticed, Mum."

A solitary diamond set in white gold had appeared on her engagement ring finger.

Angie smiled with relief. "I take it congratulations are in order."

"There's more, Mum, we're not just engaged, we're getting married... this November. We've already booked the venue. We managed to get a cancellation."

Ollie intervened. "In case you are wondering, Mrs Stewart, Charlotte is not pregnant. I just want to marry her. I'm also very fond of Joe, and Darren has been a bit slack about care recently. I think if Charlotte and I are married, it will give me a bit more authority, in case I need to step in."

"What a sensible chap you are, Ollie. Charlotte is so lucky to have you."

Angie did sometimes ask herself why Ollie put up with Charlotte. "You both, of course, have my blessing. Ollie, I think it's about time you called me Angie, don't you?"

"Or Mum?" giggled Charlotte. Ollie grinned. "I'll stick to Angie. I'm sure your mum would prefer that."

"I would. So how much is all this gonna cost?"

"We're not asking you to pay. Ollie has his inheritance, and weddings are very expensive these days."

"The one you want is," added Ollie.

"I can't wait, Mum. Joe can be a pageboy, and I've chosen the bridesmaids, and I'm hoping you'll help me with the flowers and stuff. You're good with design."

"I'll do what I can to help, Charlotte." Angie suspected that her input would largely be restricted to agreeing with everything Charlotte wanted. "Have you thought about who should give you away?" asked Angie. "If you're walking down some sort of aisle that is? I know people do things differently these days."

"We have discussed it but can't decide. Meghan Markle walked down the aisle on her own."

"Until Prince Charles stepped in," added Ollie. "It's not a church wedding, so we can do what we like really. We have to decide soon though. There's a lot to think about."

"And you are the only parent alive, so you're the only living mum or dad we can talk to." Charlotte apologised. "Sorry, that was a bit tactless, but it's how it is."

Ollie's parents and brother had been killed in a car accident, while he was still at university. Angie admired his self-reliance, but sometimes wondered whether the loss of his own parents had inflated his desire for a ready-made family. "I'll do my best to support you both. Welcome to the family, Ollie."

Ollie took Angie by surprise and kissed her on the cheek. *The second kiss on the cheek from a man in two days*, Angie reflected quietly.

"Can I give you a list of days when I need you to have Joe or do the school run? Work are letting me work flexi hours for the next month." Charlotte handed Angie a piece of paper.

"I need to check my diary. Alison will be coming out of hospital and may need me as well. I'll get back to you tomorrow."

"What would we do without you, Mrs Stewart, I mean Angie."

"I won't be able to do all the dates, Ollie, but I'll do my best." Once Ollie and Charlotte had left, Angie looked at the list. There were fifteen dates in the next four weeks. "Too much, Charlotte," Angie muttered. "I'll be exhausted. And it won't leave enough time for Alison… and Martin."

She picked up the phone and clicked on Martin's name. "I was hoping you'd ring. How did it go?"

"All good news, really, I think. She's not pregnant, and they're getting married, her and Ollie. She's wearing a beautiful engagement ring."

"Do you like him, Ollie?"

"Oh yes, he's great, and Joe adores him. God knows how he puts up with Charlotte though."

"So what's the problem?"

"Did I say there was a problem?"

"No, but I sense some doubt."

"It's going to be a big 'do', Martin, costing a lot of money and at very short notice. I forgot to ask where the reception will be, but it's bound to be somewhere expensive."

"Is the money a problem?"

"Ollie's paying. His parents and brother died in a car accident some years ago. There was insurance money and inheritance, so he can afford it. I think he feels the need to be part of a secure family."

"So shouldn't you just be happy for them?"

"I am happy for them, delighted, but Charlotte is so excited that she's on a roll. She's given me a list of fifteen days in the next month when she wants me to have Joe, so she can arrange things. Then there'll be the times she wants me to go shopping with her. When will I find time to support Alison… and see you?"

"When is the wedding?"

"This November."

"Will I get an invite?"

"Well you are family," Angie giggled.

"I can keep you company sometimes, when you have Joe, if that's acceptable, of course. An extra pair of hands is always useful, and I am CRB checked. Not that fifteen sessions in a month seems entirely reasonable. Maybe I could come over? Help you to plan?"

"When?"

"This afternoon? I won't stay late, as I'm working tomorrow."

"Okay then, come for a cup of tea. You can park round the back. Press the entry buzzer, and I'll let you in. I'm on the fourth floor."

"I'll be with you at about two."

Angie examined the flat. Apart from the morning's coffee mugs, it was tidy. She looked in the mirror and decided to wash her hair. There was just about time. The bell rang at exactly 2 pm. Martin spoke into the receiver. "This is your cousin calling."

Angie released the door. "Come on up."

A few minutes later, she heard a conversation in the lobby. She opened her front door.

"Thank you, Frank, that was very helpful. Here's Angie now." Martin stepped inside the flat and closed the door. "I have met the infamous nosy neighbour. I told him I was your cousin. These are for you." Martin handed Angie a small bunch of flowers. "To congratulate the future mother of the bride."

Angie felt tearful. "Thank you."

"Hey, you're right to feel emotional. It's a big thing, marrying off a daughter."

"And a dear friend who may be dying, and then there's you turning my emotions upside down."

"I can disappear, if you want."

"Don't you dare."

He took her hand. "So come on then, give me the guided tour." Angie led Martin into the living room. The balcony doors were still open and the afternoon sun had lit up the glass and mirrors, which Angie had strategically placed on various surfaces. "Wow, Angie, this is some flat! So much space! And I can see you have an eye for design. It looks amazing."

Martin moved over to group of hand-sewn material flowers which had been arranged in a vase in front of the fireplace. "These are beautiful. Did you make them?"

"No, I bought them in Hastings market from a young woman who makes all her own stuff. They were quite a find. Shall I take you round?" And Angie led Martin from room to room, taking care to allow him only a cursory glance in each of the three bedrooms. They returned to the kitchen, where she made tea. He carried both mugs into the living room and put them on mats on the coffee table. They sat next to each other on the large sofa.

"You have so much space. Even your hallway is larger than my living room."

"All the larger flats have massive internal halls. Some residents use their halls as office space. The only disadvantage in my hall is the lack of natural light. If the lights trip at night, the hall is really dark. I keep meaning to buy one of those round stick-on lights which run on a battery. Apart from that, they are lovely flats. The maintenance charges are a bit steep, but I don't have to worry about a thing," she grinned, "except Frank."

They settled onto the sofa, and Angie handed Charlotte's list of dates to Martin. "This is my work rota. Don't get me wrong, I love Joe, but he is tiring."

Martin looked through the list. "I suggest you take out the weekends, refuse to have Joe on a Saturday or Sunday. Weekends belong to you and me. Then remove one weekday for Alison and one for yourself. What's left?"

Angie counted. "Seven days."

"Can you cope with seven days? After all, until the schools break up, it's mainly school runs and teatime."

"Yes, of course I can. But how will I explain to Charlotte?"

"You don't have to explain. She's not your boss. Just tell her the days you can do."

Angie looked hard at Martin. "I know you're right. I need to be a bit tougher."

"It's your call, Angie. It's not my place to come between you and your daughter, but you won't be any use to her if you're exhausted. You're supposed to be retired."

"So are you, but you work."

"True, but I don't have the choice. You do." He touched her cheek. "I like your face. I want it to smile."

Angie felt a rogue tear slide down her cheek. He pressed her face into his shoulder and held her tightly. "I don't deserve you," she mumbled into his shoulder.

He stroked her cheek. "You certainly do. The question is, do I deserve you?" They lifted the mugs of tea together in silence, before Martin looked again at the amended list. He underlined three dates. "I can help with these. I'll keep them free. Will Charlotte mind?"

"She has no right to mind. You're family."

Martin laughed. "So I am. Angie, I have to go soon, got some prep to do for next week, and you need to ring Charlotte. I'll come over for my childminding booking next week, then can I see you on Saturday? This weather's going to break soon, I fear, so we ought to make the most of it."

"If you come to Bexhill on Saturday, I'll buy you a meal at my club."

"Your club?"

"You'll see." They stood up together, and he put his hand under her chin. "I can't wait any longer. I have to kiss you properly." He pulled her into a long lingering kiss, which sent unexpected ripples through her body. Martin sighed. "Gotta go now, Angie. See you at the weekend." He picked up a newspaper from beside the front door and rolled it up.

"What's that for?" enquired Angie.

"Protection against Frank." But the outside landing was deserted. "Bye, lovely. Stay strong."

Angie walked back into her flat and stepped out onto the balcony. She listened to the waves roll over the pebbles, as a hint of a breeze brushed past her cheek. She felt the calming effect of the sea. Slowly, the strong mixture of desire and anxiety which had overwhelmed her began to diminish. She went indoors and phoned Charlotte with the revised list of dates in her hand.

True to his word, Martin arrived on the Wednesday at half-past two in time for the school run. They had already agreed that they would surprise Joe by collecting him in Martin's car. "He's at an age when any different car excites him," Angie had explained. She handed Martin Joe's car seat as they walked to the lift. When they reached the car park, Stewart was embarked on his normal Wednesday car cleaning. He stopped and watched Angie and Martin approach his Fiat.

"Hi, Stewart," shouted Angie.

"Are these flats full of old men, who watch you?" whispered Martin.

"Stewart's lovely," laughed Angie, "not at all like Frank." She called over to him. "Can't stop, Stewart, on the school run."

"Joe will love the little red car." Stewart pulled a small packet of sweets from his pocket. "I've been saving these for him."

"You're so kind, Stewart."

He winked at Angie. "Well it looks like I might have a bit of competition for your affection." Stewart turned to Martin. "Look after her. She's a good'un."

Martin approached Stewart and shook his hand. "I like a man with good taste."

They found a small space close to Joe's school. "I think it might be better if I waited in the car. Give you a chance to explain that I'm with you."

"I guess you're right, and we can't have all those young mums eyeing you up and down."

"It is tempting…"

Angie kissed Martin lightly on the cheek and walked up the road to the school entrance. She waited close to a group of chattering mothers until the caretaker unlocked the tall green gate. Joe's class, known as 'Dolphins', was the third door along. He soon emerged and rushed up to Angie. "Good day?" asked Angie as they walked.

"Okay," he replied, obviously not wanting to answer questions about school.

Angie changed the subject. "I've got a surprise for you. We're going in a different car today. A friend came with me, and he's going to drive us both home."

"I have to have a car seat, Mummy says."

"I've put my car seat in his car. His name is Martin. He's nice. You'll like him. Can you see any red cars?"

Joe pointed to the little red Fiat. Martin was leaning against the side. He approached Angie and Joe and knelt down to be at Joe's level. "You okay to come in my car, Joe?"

Joe examined Martin's car. "It's very small. Where is the engine?"

Martin opened the driver door and flicked a switch releasing the catch to the bonnet. He took Joe's hand and walked him to the front of the car. "The engine's in there. It's only small, like the car."

"Can I look?"

Martin gently lifted Joe, so he could examine the engine. "What's that bit?" Joe pointed to the battery.

"That's the battery. I'll show you the rest another time. You happy to climb in the back now? Make sure you strap yourself in. Ask if you need help."

"I keep telling Grandma, I can do it by myself. I'm six now."

"Well we'll just check then, once you're strapped in, that it's tight enough. Just to keep Grandma happy."

Angie climbed into the front passenger seat, while Martin checked the harness. He slipped the packet of sweets from Stewart into Joe's hands, then sat in the front next to Angie. "You don't really need me here, do you? I feel redundant."

"I'm quite happy with car seats, but be warned, I don't do sick!"

"You'd better drive smoothly then."

"Yes, mam." Martin purposely pulled away with a jerk, and Joe laughed. Angie looked worried.

"Don't worry, Angie, that's the one and only time I will do that with Joe in the car. I promise. But I have to warn you, the suspension in the back is a bit harsh."

True to his word, Martin drove slowly and carefully back to Angie's flat. They had two hours before Joe's dad, Darren, was due to collect Joe for the night. Martin had a natural way with children, and paid Joe attention without overpowering him. Three games of cards, a cooked tea of sausage and chips and one episode of *Horrid Henry* on TV soon passed the time. The doorbell rang, and Angie opened it for Darren. Joe grabbed his bag and rushed to his dad. "Hi, Joe, have you had a nice time with Grandma?"

"And with Martin, he showed me the engine in his red car."

Martin appeared in the hallway and shook Darren's hand. "Hi, I'm Angie's cousin."

Joe's dad did not seem interested in Martin. "Come on Joe, I'm in a hurry."

Joe waved. "Bye Grandma, bye Martin."

"I'll see you next week," Angie shouted after Joe.

They walked into the kitchen, and Angie bent down to pick up a couple of stray chips from the floor. "That seemed to go well," she remarked to Martin.

"It did, didn't it, but I'm used to kids. It does help. His dad doesn't say much, does he? Will he mind my being here?"

"I doubt he'll even think about it. I'm much more worried about what Charlotte will think... and before you say anything, it won't make any difference what she thinks. Joe really liked you, and you were good with him." Once again, Martin kissed Angie goodbye, headed back to Eastbourne and left her alone in the flat to reflect on the past few hours.

CHAPTER TWELVE

The Storm

Martin arrived mid-afternoon on Saturday. Not wishing to appear forward, he had left his overnight bag in his car. She buzzed him in, and he was soon standing in her hallway. "For you."

"More flowers?"

"I am male. When it comes to gifts, my imagination is limited, but I have brought wine as well. Are we allowed to drink it on the balcony?"

"Unless the wine is attached to a line of washing, we certainly are." Angie fetched some glasses, while Martin unscrewed the bottle. They sat and watched the coloured sailing boats which were taking advantage of the warm afternoon. "There's a storm forecast, but no sign of it yet. During the last fierce storm, we lost all power for an hour. It was quite scary."

"Mr Black will look after you. He's good in the dark. What time are we heading to this club place?"

"About half-past four. They have live music on the terrace for two hours or so, then I have booked a table for dinner. You will have to let me pay though. It's booked in my name, a thank you for helping with Joe." Angie was aware that Martin's funds were not unlimited.

She disappeared into her bedroom and changed, while Martin

brought in the glasses and half-empty bottle of wine. He locked the balcony doors and watched her approach. "Blimey!"

Angie was wearing a loose-fitting pale blue summer dress with shoulder straps. She knew it showed her figure to advantage. "I am one lucky man. Do I need a tie?"

"Absolutely not. What you're wearing is fine."

They walked along Bexhill seafront hand in hand. The weather and tides had conspired to provide the perfect conditions for a romantic evening. The early evening sun was already sending rose-pink reflections across the sand which had been revealed by the low tide. Seagulls swooped in circles, lifted by the thermals. They could hear the faint sound of a saxophone coming from the direction of The Club. "Hi Angie," she was greeted by several groups of walkers.

"You seem to know a lot of people."

"That's Bexhill for you. Now they will all return home and discuss who you might be."

Just beyond the De La Warr Pavilion car park was a short unremarkable road which led down to the seafront. Angie turned the corner and stepped into a tiled open porch. She took a plastic engraved key fob from her bag and held it up to a small button. The front door clicked open. "What is this? MI5 headquarters?"

"You'll see."

Martin found himself in a well-appointed hallway with polished floorboards and traditional seating. A digital display announced that they were in The Club at the Waterfront. Angie signed Martin in as a guest, and he followed her down a short staircase through a hotel-style bar and lounge. This led to a large outdoor patio overlooking the English Channel. A young saxophonist was playing in the background. They were shown to a seat under a large umbrella. The waiter seemed to recognise Angie and took her order for drinks. "Yet another surprise from my cousin of the year. How on earth did you find out about this place? Is it expensive?"

"Not especially. A lot of people in Bexhill belong."

"Are there rules? I mean is one allowed to hold hands with the members?"

"Only with permission, which I give you." Angie reached out and took Martin's hand.

There was much to discuss, Charlotte's marriage, Jessica's new job and Angie's relationship with Robin. "How can someone who ran betting shops be so straight-laced?"

"Turf Accountant, please! He was always trying to prove that he was respectable. He wasn't unkind to me Martin, just... unimaginative. And he spoiled Charlotte, because he wanted her approval. All the tough stuff was left to me."

The time passed quickly. A few dark clouds began to settle in the distance, and the heat started to build. The waiter approached their table. "Are you ready to eat? I've set a table for you in the restaurant. We're expecting rain later."

They moved indoors to the restaurant and continued the conversation. The air pressure was deepening and repressed their appetites, so they only ate a small main course each. Angie gave the waiter her card. They finished their wine and began to walk slowly back to West Parade. The atmosphere was oppressive, and the sky was growing darker. A faint rumbling of thunder could be heard in the distance. Martin led Angie to a bench just across the road from her flat. The seafront had emptied, and he took her face in his hands. He kissed her repeatedly. "It's lovely here. I don't want to go in yet." He kissed her again, this time slipping his hand on her knee under her dress. They were totally absorbed in each other. Neither of them noticed the blackening sky which had formed above them.

There was a loud crash of thunder, and a fork of lightning flashed into the sea. The dark clouds immediately sent golf balls of rain directly down onto them. Within seconds there were rivers of water flowing down the road. There was no escape. They were completely drenched.

Martin grabbed Angie's hand as the lightning grew closer. "We have to get inside."

"Head round the back," Angie shouted, "I'll follow you." By the time they were in the foyer, their clothes were saturated. They called the lift and dripped their way inside.

"I'm sorry, I should have seen this coming," apologised Martin.

They stood wet through on the hallway carpet in the flat. Angie grabbed a towelling dressing gown from the spare room and handed it to Martin. "Use the bathroom." She disappeared into her bedroom and slowly peeled off her dripping clothes. She just had time to towel dry her hair and put on a satin dressing gown before there was a massive flash and an ear-piercing bang. The lights went out. Night-time had descended suddenly and, apart from the occasional burst of lightning, there was no natural light from outside. The flat was plunged into complete darkness. Angie opened the bedroom door.

She heard Martin's voice. "Angie, are you okay?"

"Yes, we've been struck. It's happened before. The emergency lighting should come on in the landing soon."

"Where are you? I can't see a thing."

"I'm standing in my bedroom doorway."

"Stay where you are. I will feel my way around the walls and find you. Keep talking so I know when you are close." She soon sensed his hands touching her shoulder. "Which bit of you is that?"

"My shoulder."

"Shame." He manoeuvred himself in front of her and slipped one arm underneath her dressing gown around her waist. "This is definitely you, is it?" Her dressing gown had fallen open, and he was aware of her naked breasts against his chest.

"Maybe you should have a feel around, and check."

Martin slowly ran his hands over her breasts. His mouth and hands began to explore her body in the darkness. "I'm not yet sure it's you. I need to feel some more."

She felt his fingers stroke her nipples while he kissed her repeatedly before finally resting one hand at the top of her leg. "Christ, you are beautiful. I want you so much."

Angie gasped, "Could we sit down?" Martin removed his dressing gown and rolled it into a pillow. He lowered Angie towards it and laid her down on the hall carpet, kissing her mouth and her body repeatedly. "You are my perfect woman." By the time they joined together she was desperate to receive him. The length and depth of the climax between them took them both by surprise. When they finally drew apart, they were both exhausted by what had passed.

There was a knock on the door. "Angie, are you all right? I heard loud banging from your hallway. I thought someone cried out."

Angie repressed a giggle. "I'm fine, Frank. My cousin is here looking after me." Martin ran his lips over her nipples while she spoke, and she gently pushed him away.

"Well, just let me know if you need anything. The emergency lighting is on out here, and several of us are meeting at my place with a torch."

"I'm fine, Frank, really. You go back to your flat."

"As long as you're sure?"

"I'm sure." Angie whispered to Martin, "I bet he's listening outside the door. Look, I'm very uncomfortable on this floor. Whenever the lighting flashes, I can just see my bed. Do you think we could crawl there?"

"Let's go for it."

"Follow me." They slowly crawled in line through Angie's bedroom and helped each other climb onto the bed. The darkness was punctuated by intermittent flashes of lightning.

"This is some storm!" exclaimed Martin. A few minutes later, he kissed Angie again. "Angie, if you say no, I will understand, but I can't stop wanting you. Do you think we might make love again? I realise a bed is rather traditional, but I'll do my best to excite you."

"I thought you'd never ask."

The power came back on at 2 am. The flat was suddenly flooded in light, and Angie found herself lying naked on top of her bed. Martin was asleep, but his arm was resting across her body. She felt exposed and slowly sat up, pulling the bedcover over herself. Martin woke and turned towards her. "Hello, lovely, are you okay?"

Angie yawned, "Just a bit stiff. Actually, I ache all over."

"We did rather go for it last night, didn't we?" He kissed her gently. "You were wonderful. You are wonderful." Angie warmed to the much-needed compliment.

"You want tea?" asked Martin.

"Milk, no sugar."

"I remember." Martin stood up, walked into the hallway and picked up their dressing gowns. He slipped his on, and dropped the other one on Angie's bed. "Where's your fuse box?"

"In the hall cupboard."

"I'll check nothing has shorted." He opened the hall cupboard and examined the trip switches. "All looks fine."

Angie was aware of Martin wandering around the flat turning off lights, before she heard him in the kitchen making tea. He appeared with two mugs. "Thank you."

"You are very welcome." He slipped his arm under the bedclothes and took her hand.

"There's something I need to say." Angie felt anxious. "Actually, there are two things, but the other can wait 'til tomorrow."

"Should I be worried?"

"I hope not, Angie. What I want to say now is that, last night, well it was amazing, wasn't it, and I thought we were rather splendid. The storm and the evening and the pent-up emotion that I felt for you seemed to transform me into a young man again. I just want to remind you that I am sixty-three years old. I may not always be able to produce quite such a testosterone-filled performance. I wouldn't want you to raise your expectations too high. What I mean is, I'm not getting any younger."

Angie laughed. "It was incredible. I loved every sex-filled minute. I've never had an experience like it before, not ever. And now my back aches, my legs hurt, my neck is stiff, and I'm having trouble lifting this tea mug. I think we need to take things a bit more gently next time."

"You do want there to be a next time?"

"I do, but I might need some recovery time."

Martin turned off the bedside light, wrapped her in his arms, and they both drifted back to sleep.

CHAPTER THIRTEEN

Eastbourne

Angie woke again at 9 am to hear Martin in the kitchen. She slipped on her dressing gown and walked to the door. "I'm trying to prove I can be domestic as well as a stud. I wasn't sure if you put your posh glasses in the dishwasher, so I've washed them up," explained Martin.

"Everything goes in the dishwasher, but thank you, Martin. Are your clothes dry?"

"No, they're hanging in the bathroom, still damp."

"I do have a tumble drier."

"Not necessary, there's an overnight bag in my car with a spare set of clothes in it."

"You were planning on staying then."

"I hoped. I wondered if you would mind getting the bag from my car. I think Frank might have a heart attack if he sees me in your dressing gown."

Angie laughed. "I couldn't believe it when he knocked. D'you think he heard us?"

"He probably held an ear trumpet against the door."

Angie dressed slowly, and quickly brushed her hair. She added a faint touch of lipstick. "Give me your keys."

"My car is near to the rear entrance. The bag's in the boot."

As Angie stepped outside into the rear car park, Frank was hovering. "Morning, Angie."

"Morning, Frank, that was some storm, wasn't it?"

"Lucky you had some company. Is that his Fiat?"

"It is."

"Not good to leave a car out in this weather, especially an old one. If ever he needs to use my garage, you only have to ask."

"That's very kind of you, Frank."

Angie grabbed the bag from Martin's car and returned to her flat. "Frank was hovering. He wants to lend you his garage."

"So he can keep an eye on me, no doubt."

"He'll do that whatever. I'm sorry about Frank. He's irritating, but harmless."

"A bit like me then. Where should I get dressed?"

"Use my bedroom." Angie liked the familiarity of Martin dressing in her room. He took his bag through and put on a dry set of clothes. "What do you do about breakfast?"

"Toast here, or a bacon roll on the seafront? I make good coffee."

"Let's do toast and coffee here then. I have something else I need to run by you."

Angie's heart quickened. "Oh yes, I forgot."

The air was fresh after the storm, but it was too damp to sit on the balcony. They sat at Angie's small kitchen table with toast and coffee. "Fire away. Don't keep me in suspense."

"You'll think I'm rushing ahead of myself, but I need to say this now. I know it's too early to think about 'us', long-term I mean, but as far as I'm concerned that's what I want. I knew from the moment I saw you at Jack's funeral, and it's not as if we need to check out each other's background." Angie started to speak, but Martin interrupted. "Let me finish. There's more. I know you'll need time. You're careful, less impulsive than me, most women are, and that's fine. I'm not trying to rush you, but there is a problem, Angie. I'm poor, no not poor, but not especially well-off. I own a tatty terraced house in Eastbourne, run a clapped-out Fiat, and I survive on my teacher's pension. The supply work pays for a few extras, but I could never afford expensive holidays or joining posh clubs. Most of my eating out is restricted to takeaways with Jess. I know you have money, but I don't want to be a kept man."

"Can I speak now?"

"Yes."

"Would it be different if you were the woman and I was the man?"

"I wouldn't fancy you half as much."

Angie smiled. "You know what I mean."

"I do, Angie, but I'm from a generation when these things do matter. Other people will make judgements as well."

"This is not the business of other people." Angie was thoughtful. "I respect you for being honest, and, bluntly, I'm not going to change my lifestyle just to make you feel better. This is a problem in your head, Martin, not mine."

He took her hand. "I'm sure I'll get over it. I just needed to say."

"Are you busy today? Can we visit your house in Eastbourne?"

"Must we?"

"Let's purge the gremlins. If you don't mind coming back here after, I'll drive."

Dishwasher loaded, they took the lift to the ground floor. Martin followed Angie to a garage, which she opened with a remote control to reveal a top of the range BMW. "I knew it!"

"What d'you mean?"

"BMW Seven Series, the opposite of a clapped-out Fiat."

"Stop complaining, and get in. I'd offer to let you drive, but you're not insured." Angie reversed out of the garage, and remotely closed the door.

"Give me directions when we get this side of Eastbourne, will you?"

Martin was surprised at the skill with which she handled the car but decided not to comment. They were soon turning into a narrow road of terraced houses just outside of Eastbourne town centre. "You might have problems finding a space. I normally park in front of my house, but I'm not sure your car will fit."

"Is this your house?"

"Yep."

"You watch."

Angie turned on the parking sensor, and carefully reversed onto the hard standing in front of Martin's house.

"Is there nothing you can't do?"

Angie grinned. "You won't be able to get out easily though."

"I'll manage." With great determination, he carefully opened the car door, twisted himself through the narrow gap, and walked to his front entrance. Angie followed. The open door revealed a tiny hall which led directly into a living area. It was clean, but over-furnished, with two bookcases, an obviously second-hand table and chairs, and an old-fashioned three-piece suite.

"I see your lack of funds didn't make you skimp on the TV." Angie pointed to the modern 60-inch flat screen TV, which was mounted on the wall.

"A man must have some toys to while away his lonely evenings."

Angie walked into the kitchen. "Somewhat bijou, but functional. You'd have more space if you bought a wall-mounted dishwasher."

"God, you take a woman to bed, and she thinks it gives her the right to squeeze you into a BMW and reorganise your kitchen. Any other criticisms?"

"I haven't been upstairs yet."

"I'll make you a cuppa, while you explore. I don't think I want to witness any more of your comments."

Angie climbed the open plan staircase which led to two upstairs bedrooms and a bathroom. "Only one loo," she muttered. "That's inconvenient." She headed back downstairs, and Martin handed her a mug of tea.

"I did warn you."

"Martin, I don't judge people by the houses they live in. You're right, it is small, but it's kinda cute. I could transform this place into an ideal home exhibition for about £500. Not that I think you'd want me to."

"I temporarily forgot that you're an interior designer. I feel even worse now. Drink your tea and stop staring at everything." Angie couldn't help herself. She prowled around the house opening cupboards and checking for original features.

"You're making me feel uncomfortable."

"Sorry." Angie sat down. "It's a nice little house, bachelor-ish and a bit tatty, but that's what you told me to expect. I think I'd be worried if it was too beautiful. It wouldn't seem right." Angie picked up a framed photograph. "Is this Jess?"

"Yes."

"She has your good looks."

Martin was pleased. "I'd like you to meet her."

"I'd like that too."

They drank their tea. Martin took the empty mugs into the kitchen. "You stay in here. There really isn't room for two in my kitchen, and in any case you'd only criticise my dishwasher."

Angie grinned. "I don't think you'd believe me, if I said your house was spacious and charming. It's cramped and a bit chaotic. But you've not been with anyone to want to turn it into a home. You've had no incentive. It doesn't make a difference, Martin, about us, I mean."

He kissed her lightly. "It worries me."

She pulled him towards her and kissed him properly. "Try not to let it, please. We'll find a way through." Angie wondered if Martin might use the differential in their income to keep a distance between them... to maintain a lack of commitment.

He seemed to read her thoughts. "I won't let this come between us, I promise. Now would you mind driving your car out of the front, before I try to climb in again?"

She smiled. "Whatever you say."

They chatted easily on the return journey. "Are you working tomorrow?"

"No, I try not to accept work on Mondays. It gives me a three-day break. The schools finish soon, anyway."

"So do you have to go back tonight?" Angie felt a bit pushy.

"If you'd like me to stay, I'll stay. You should've said before. I'd have grabbed some more stuff."

"I didn't like to ask."

"I'd love to stay. Have you got food in? We missed lunch. Should we stop at a shop?"

"I'm okay without lunch, if you are. Maybe we could buy a few bits for dinner?" The idea of cooking together appealed to them both.

Frank watched them from his window, as they carried the shopping bags into the lobby. "He's there again, Frank the observer. Does he fancy you?"

"I honestly don't think so. He's just nosy, and he hasn't lived here long. He seems to want to be in charge. He'll wait until you're not around and start asking me questions. I thought I might tell him you're a drug dealer and just released from prison."

"Tempting, but don't you dare!" They prepared a casserole, Martin happy to take his instructions from Angie. Then they sat on the balcony and watched the evening sun descend. Martin fetched some glasses and a bottle of wine. "You see, I already know where the important things are in your flat." He suddenly started to laugh. "In fact, I could find my way around in complete darkness." An easy atmosphere settled between them.

"Martin, I need to ask you something."

"Will it hurt?"

"I very much doubt it."

"Go on then."

"Have you got any points on your driving licence?"

"Not at present. What is this, the Spanish Inquisition?"

"Would you mind if I insured you to drive my car?"

"Because you don't like being a passenger in mine?"

"No, stupid. It just might make things less complicated with you helping me with Joe, and maybe other stuff as well. I don't think my life's going to be easy in the next few months."

"So let me get this right. You want to insure me to drive your top of the range BMW and claim it is to make your life easier."

"That's about it, yep."

"And you wonder why I like you so much?"

"I'll take that as a yes then. We'll ring the insurance tomorrow."

Martin was reluctant to leave Angie and return to Eastbourne. He sensed that she was still feeling insecure about his intentions. It had caused him problems with women in the past. They had been interested in him, but tended to interpret his easy wit as an indication that he might be a bit of a 'player'. It didn't help that his infidelity had ruined his marriage, and Angie was definitely not the sort of woman you could placate with a few clever phrases. Despite his concerns about the disparity in their income, he was enormously attracted to Angie and genuinely believed they could build a future together. He wasn't getting any younger, and it felt like a last chance to settle down. He would need to work hard to make this happen. He sat at the breakfast table on the Monday morning and watched her take bites of toast. Angie felt uncomfortable. "Do you have to scrutinise me while I'm eating?"

"Sorry, I was just enjoying sharing breakfast. I've been on my own for too long."

Angie stopped eating. "When Robin died, I mean once I got over the grief, I quite enjoyed living on my own for a while, making my own decisions. I'd always had a lot of independence, work-wise, but Robin liked to rule our domestic situation."

Martin took a risk. "You don't strike me as someone who would be subservient in a marriage. You come across as rather assertive. I can't imagine you playing the role of the little woman."

"I mostly just gave in, Martin. It's no fun arguing all the time. But I'm different now. I like having more control. Is that a problem for you?"

He grinned. "Schools are full of bossy women. I'm used to it."

Angie looked worried. "Am I really that bossy?"

Martin reached over to Angie's plate and took a bite of Angie's toast. "Nothing I can't handle. I like a challenge." He handed back the half-eaten toast. "I will have to go home after lunch though. I'm working for the last two days of term, and I've got to do a bit of prep. I'm also running out of clothes." Martin noticed Angie's look of disappointment. "Have you got Joe on Wednesday?"

"Yes, just for a couple of hours."

"I'd be happy to come over and help after work, if you want. Then later, I wondered if you'd like to meet Jess? She starts her new job soon, so may not have so much time after that."

"I'd like that. Does she know about me?"

"I might just have mentioned you a few times," Martin grinned. "We could drop Joe off and then drive to Eastbourne to meet Jess. It would give me a chance to drive your car."

"Sounds like a plan."

CHAPTER FOURTEEN

The Tea Party

Within hours of Martin returning to Eastbourne, the time began to drag, and Angie found herself longing for the school holidays. She didn't actually know how often Martin would stay with her, but she began to occupy herself by making lists of possible meals he might like. Her list-making was interrupted by a phone call from Alison's sister. "How is she?" Angie asked. "Are you back home?"

"The hospital signed her off an hour ago, and we've just got home. Alison is resting, and she made me promise I'd ring you. She wants you to come over for tea tomorrow afternoon."

"Tea? That doesn't sound like Alison."

"She's been off the booze for over five days. I don't think that's helping her mood."

Angie laughed. "Can I bring anything? D'you need any shopping?"

"We're fine. I'm going shopping in a minute. Alison has given me a long list."

"That's nice for you. I'll see you tomorrow then."

Susan's call jolted Angie into action, and she wrote a shopping list for herself. Filling her cupboards with food would provide a useful distraction. She spent the rest of the afternoon on an excursion to the supermarket. When she had finally carried the last of the bags from her car into the lift, Angie began to feel tired. As she approached her front door, Frank appeared. "You could do with that lodger of yours here to help with your shopping." Angie couldn't be bothered to argue. She lifted the last of her bags into her flat and slammed the door in Frank's face. There was an ansaphone message from Martin waiting for her.

I dunno, I leave you for a few hours, and you're already out gallivanting. Bet you're not missing me at all. If you can spare the time, give me a ring. I want to hear your voice.

Angie phoned him straightaway. "Hello, Martin, this is Angie's voice."

"Hello, Angie's voice, have you been anywhere nice?"

"Shopping, in case you reappear."

"I'll have to come then. We mustn't waste your shopping. Is everything okay?"

"Sort of. Alison's out of hospital, and I've been invited for tea tomorrow. That is SO not Alison."

"Perhaps it's her sister's idea?" Martin suggested.

"Maybe, just feels a bit odd. I normally buy her a bottle, but I've bought a cake instead."

"Try not to worry, sweetheart, I'm sure things will be fine. Shame I'm working tomorrow, I'd like to meet her."

"She is desperate to meet you!"

"We'll do that soon then, if she's well enough. No news, I s'pose?"

"Susan, her sister, said very little, just the tea invitation."

They both tried to keep the conversation going. "I'm lonely here without you," said Martin. "I hope we can spend a bit more time together once the schools break up."

"So do I, and of course I'll need your help eating up all my shopping."

"I'll get away from work as soon as I can on Wednesday. Should be with you by about 4.30 latest. After we get back from meeting Jess, can I stay over?" Martin asked.

"You really don't have to ask, of course you can." Angie was pleased.

"I don't like to presume. You might have plans."

"Nothing that can't include you, Martin, and if I do make a rare visit to a client, it normally only takes a couple of hours." They were running out of things to say.

"Ring me just before you go to sleep, will you?" Martin asked. Angie agreed, and the call was ended.

She put the last of her shopping away before grabbing a sandwich and turning on the TV.

Later that evening, once she was ready for bed, Angie phoned Martin back. "Hello?" A female voice answered Martin's phone.

Angie was startled. "Is Martin there?"

"He's in the bathroom. This is Jess, his daughter. I just popped in to borrow a screwdriver. Is that Angie?"

"It is. Hello, Jess, I believe we're meeting up on Wednesday."

"That's right, I'm looking forward to it. Oh, here's Dad now."

Angie heard Jessica's voice talking to Martin in the distance.

He came on the phone. "Sorry about that. She's gone now. She treats me like her personal branch of B and Q. It must have thrown you when a female voice answered the phone."

"It did."

He laughed. "She's bought a flat pack chest of drawers and needed a Philips screwdriver. I'll probably have to rebuild it when I next go round."

"I guess it's good that our grown-up kids still need us, even if it is just for child-minding and furniture building."

Martin changed the subject. "Are you in bed?"

"No, I'm in the living room."

"Shame, I wanted to imagine you in bed."

Angie found herself blushing. "You'll have to wait for the real thing."

"Okay, sweetheart, I'll let you off, but don't stay up late, you need to be strong for Alison. I won't have time to ring you before

I go to work tomorrow, but should be home by five. Will you ring me and let me know the news after your tea party?"

"I will," she promised. They ended the call.

The following day Martin texted Angie at lunchtime.

Hope all goes well this afternoon xx

Thank you xx

Angie knocked on Alison's door at precisely 3 pm. She was carrying a large wrapped cake and a bunch of flowers. Susan answered the door. "Come through." Alison was sitting in an armchair. In front of her was a table full of sandwiches and cakes. She stood up slowly and hugged her friend. "You don't need to get up, Alison," Angie protested.

"I do. Every minute of every day is important from now on." Angie gave Susan a worried look, but Alison carried on talking. "Now we have smoked salmon, and chocolate spread sandwiches, and cream cakes, and your special cake, and two types of tea."

Angie pulled a face. "Chocolate spread!"

"I'd never tasted it, so wanted to try. It's horrible. Take the rest of the tub home for Joe."

Angie giggled. "I'll have the smoked salmon then and a cup of Earl Grey." Susan poured the tea.

Angie looked puzzled. "This tea party thing is very 'not you', Alison. Are you sure they didn't operate on your brain?"

"My thinking is crystal clear. I have never before in my life hosted a tea party, so I decided it would be the first of all the new experiences I wanted to try. This is my version of twenty things you must do before you die." Angie tried not to look too concerned. Alison continued, "I've made a decision, you see." She reached out and took her sister's hand. "I'm not having any more chemo. They gave me a massive internal dose at the hospital, but I'm not having any more." She looked at her friend. "There's no point in trying to make me change my mind. Even with chemo, my odds of survival are not good, and I'm not going to put up with any more invasive treatment. They've removed the lumps and they think they can keep the cancer under control with medication for a few months. Then they can fill me full of morphine, and I will quietly slip away. In the meantime, I'm going to live it up on my version of chocolate spread." Angie felt her eyes begin to well up so she turned her back on Alison and looked out of the window. "I want no tears, Angie. I'm one of the lucky ones. I get to make a few more decisions before I go. I might even make it to that daughter of yours' wedding, if she'll have me."

Angie threw her arms around her friend. "I'm sure she would love you to come." She felt a tear trickle down her cheek.

Alison beckoned to her sister. "For God's sake, fetch her a tissue."

"I'm sorry, Alison, I just didn't expect this. You've always been such a fighter."

"And a realist. I know my time has come."

Angie pressed her nails into her knuckles to prevent anymore tears. "Please tell me you're allowed to start drinking alcohol again."

"From this Friday. And I expect you to bring Mr Sexy Cousin round to celebrate with me as soon as possible."

Angie turned to Susan. "How long are you staying?"

"Probably just a couple more days to give Alison time to become a bit more mobile. But I'll keep popping back." The trio sat around the table, and each took a cream cake. When Angie finally left, it was almost 6 pm.

She drove home and texted Martin.

Will phone soon. Not good news but probably for the best x

Once she had regained control of her emotions, Angie phoned Martin and described her afternoon in detail. She then phoned Charlotte to give her the news. "Of course Alison can come to the wedding, Mum."

CHAPTER FIFTEEN

Jess Meets Angie

Angie was woken up by a text on Wednesday morning. It was from Charlotte.

Have you remembered you're doing the school run today?

Angie texted back.

Yes all organised.

It's the last day of term so he'll have extra stuff. Will that man be with you?

Angie wanted to avoid more conflict. She should really have explained to Charlotte about Martin, but as it was Darren who last picked Joe up, she had avoided the subject.

If you mean Martin then for part of the time, yes. I assume that's okay? We'll drop Joe off at about 6.

Several minutes passed before Charlotte replied.

I'm not happy about it, but I guess it will have to be OK.

Angie decided not to respond.

Joe looked disappointed when Angie led him to her own car after school. "I thought it would be the red car again. Mummy said that man would be coming."

"And can you remember that man's name, Joe?" Angie tried not to sound annoyed.

"Of course, I can. It's Martin. Ollie says he's your boyfriend."

Angie laughed. "I suppose he is. He's coming to the flat a bit later, when he leaves work."

"That's good, because we need three players at cards."

Martin arrived at the flat at about 4.30 pm. Angie buzzed him in and stood waiting at the flat door with Joe. He put down his bag and kissed her lightly on the cheek. "You got away from work quickly," said Angie.

"I couldn't wait any longer."

Joe grabbed Martin by the hand and pulled him towards the table in the living room where he had set out the cards. "Bit of a busman's holiday, this, Joe!"

"I thought you were a teacher. Do you drive a bus as well?"

"No, Joe, it's just an expression. I'll explain another day. Now which pile is mine?"

Joe pointed to each pile of cards. "That's mine, that's Grandma's, and that's Grandpa Martin's."

Martin gave Angie a quizzical look. She held out her hands and shrugged her shoulders.

They played cards until tea-time, then watched Joe eat before preparing to drop him off.

Charlotte was looking out for them through the front window.

"He's only driving her car! I hope he's insured."

"He's bound to be," reassured Ollie. "Your mum's really careful about that sort of thing. You should go out and say hello."

"I can't. You do it."

Ollie walked out and opened the back door of Angie's car to release Joe. Martin climbed out and held out his hand to Ollie. Ollie shook Martin's hand warmly. "You're very privileged. She's never let me drive it." Martin grinned.

Angie got out of the car. "Is Charlotte coming out?"

"She's cooking," lied Ollie. "Come on Joe. Make sure you've got everything, then we can go in. Say goodbye to Grandma and Martin."

Joe gave a wave. "Bye Grandma, bye Martin. Thank you for having me."

Martin pulled away, and Angie grinned. "I see you've been demoted back to just 'Martin'. Where on earth did the name 'Grandpa Martin' come from?"

"I have no idea, but I did rather like it. Children of his age are always trying to make sense of their world. I'm guessing calling me 'Grandpa' was Joe's way of linking us together. Should I stop him?"

"Certainly not. It's great that he's taken to you so easily. He's showing a lot more maturity than his mother."

Martin decided to change the subject. "Ollie seems okay."

"He is. I really like him."

Martin had arranged to meet Jessica at an Italian restaurant on Eastbourne Marina. He thought it would be quieter than a pub and he wanted her to have a chance to chat to Angie. Angie felt nervous as Martin parked his car in the large car park. The previous weekend's storm had freshened the air, and she wrapped a soft pashmina around her shoulders to protect against the evening breeze. Jessica was already seated in the restaurant. She watched Martin put his hand on the back of Angie's shoulder and lead her towards Jessica's table. Angie looked strikingly elegant, and heads turned to look at her. Jessica had met a number of her father's female acquaintances in the past, but had never seen him so attentive. She stood up, kissed her father, then gave Angie a tentative hug. "It's great to meet you." They sat down and took refuge from stilted conversation by examining the menus. Angie and Martin had already agreed that Martin would pay. He ordered a bottle of wine, and a shandy for himself.

"Jess lives quite near, so walked here, but I promised I'd drop her off on our way home."

"And get to ride in the famous car!" Jessica grinned.

"That's the only way I can keep him, Jess, by bribing him with my car."

"It doesn't look that way to me, Angie. I've never known him to talk so much about a woman. I'm hopeful that at last there's a chance someone will take him off my hands. He's far too much responsibility for me."

Angie was disarmed by Jessica. She had a look of her father and swept her long hair off her face in a similar manner. She had also definitely inherited his charisma. "Is he really that troublesome, Jess? I may need some tips about how to deal with him."

Martin grinned. "Would you both like me to leave, so you can talk in private?"

"We need you to drive us home," said both women in unison, then burst out laughing.

Martin ordered a second bottle of wine. "I hope you're not working tomorrow, Jess."

"I finished at Channel View today, Dad. I've got four days off, before I start my new job."

Martin had always enjoyed female company and watching the banter between Angie and his daughter filled him with joy. He slipped his hand affectionately on Angie's knee while the women conversed. Jessica told Angie about her new job, and then Angie described some of her experiences as an interior designer. "You should take on Dad's house in Eastbourne. It's a design disaster, not helped by that ridiculously large TV. Have you been there yet?"

Martin rolled his eyes. "She's already tried to redesign my kitchen, Jess."

Angie took a pen out of her bag and began to draw a square on the paper placemat. She turned the paper upside down so Jessica could see it. "This is his kitchen. He's got that bloody great dishwasher there, taking up far too much space. If he put a wall-mounted dishwasher here, he could move the washer drier under the worktop and free up so much room." The women continued to exclude Martin from the conversation until the waiter brought food and a new paper placemat.

"There really isn't a lot of point me doing up my house, while I'm spending so much time at Angie's," Martin interrupted.

"That's true, Dad, I s'pose." The women gave Martin a break from talking about him, while they ate their food. By the time Martin paid the bill, Angie and Jessica felt like old friends. They were also both slightly drunk. Each clung on to Martin's arm as they walked with him to the car. "So this is the famous car," Jessica's speech was slightly slurred. Martin drove carefully to her house. It was one of a row of modern townhouses further along the harbour. He helped his daughter out of the car. "Will you be all right on your own, Jess? You've had a fair amount to drink."

"Stop fussing, Dad, I'll be fine." Angie and Martin watched as Jessica found her key and managed to let herself in.

He drove round the corner and stopped the car. Angie felt concerned, but Martin lent over and kissed her. "I've been wanting to do that all evening."

Angie hiccupped, "You shouldn't take advantage of a woman who's been drinking."

"That can wait 'til I get you home." Martin started the engine and pressed hard on the accelerator. He hoped Angie was too drunk to notice the speedometer.

CHAPTER SIXTEEN

The Wedding Co-ordinator

Jessica arrived at her new job full of optimism. She was wearing a long cashmere jumper over tailored black trousers. "Dress smartly, but not too formal," Felicity had advised. "Some of our brides to be are quite nervous, and they need to regard you as a friend. The more they relate to you, the more they will spend."

Jessica swept back her long hair, as she walked into the timber-beamed hallway. Felicity came out to greet her. She shook Jessica by the hand. "Welcome to Belmont Grange." Jessica followed Felicity into the office. "I'm sorry to do this to you on your first morning, but I have some clients for you to see on your own. My mum's been rushed into hospital, and I have to go and see her. The couple have already booked their date in November, and paid the deposit, but they want to go through a few details. The bride seems quite young, but she is definitely in charge. I know I went through the folder with you on your induction afternoon, but, if you can't answer anything, don't guess, tell them you will email."

"What time are they booked in?"

"About 10 after they've dropped off their son. They have a six-year-old called Joe. I think he'll be a pageboy."

Jessica looked at her watch. It was 9.15. "Leave it with me. I'll be fine. You need to be with your mum."

Jessica thought she saw Felicity blink away a tear. "Thank you. I knew you were the right person for this job. Ask Tina to serve coffee, when they arrive." Felicity grabbed her handbag and mobile and left the building.

Jessica took her folder out of her shoulder bag, and began to flick through each section. She had read it so many times, she practically knew it off by heart. "Better safe, than sorry," she said quietly.

Just before ten, she heard a bell ring from the reception area. An attractive young girl with long blonde hair and a slightly older-looking man were standing in the hallway. Jessica held out her hand to Ollie. "Mr Jeffreys... and it's Charlotte, isn't it? Welcome to Belmont Grange. I'm Jessica Black, the wedding co-ordinator. If it's okay with you, I thought we'd go and sit in the drawing room and have a coffee first. I can then walk you round the different rooms to discuss how you want to use the space."

"That sounds great," replied Ollie, aware that Charlotte was pre-occupied with soaking up the atmosphere. Jessica stood beside her.

"It's a wonderful venue for a wedding, isn't it? And if you don't mind me saying you will make a really beautiful bride." Charlotte smiled, and Ollie looked at her affectionately. Making full use of the charm she had inherited from her father, Jessica began to draw the couple into her confidence. "So how many guests, approximately?"

"About eighty for the wedding, and another eighty or so in the evening."

"And you've taken the option to book the whole hotel for the night? I think that's wise, then you can make as much noise as you want without worrying." Coffee was served, while Jessica slowly went through each detail in the folder. "We can arrange a taster afternoon, so you can both sample the menu. What about your parents, will they want to be involved?"

Ollie interrupted. "My parents died when I was quite young, and Charlotte's dad died a few years ago, so there's only Charlotte's mum left now."

"Well, the mother of the bride is an important role. Will she be on her own?"

"She doesn't have a partner, if that's what you mean," replied Charlotte.

"She might by then," Ollie grinned. "She's got a boyfriend. I expect she'll want him invited."

"Not if I can help it," interrupted Charlotte.

Jessica looked concerned. "I take it you don't like him."

"She's never met him." Ollie shook his head.

"I just don't like the idea of someone replacing my dad. And she's too old to have a boyfriend anyway."

"We'll just leave that one on hold for the time being then, shall we? Charlotte, do you want to arrange for your mum to visit Belmont Grange before the wedding?"

"Is that normal?" asked Charlotte.

"In my experience most mothers of the bride do like to get involved."

Charlotte looked surprised. "I'll ask her then."

Feeling that she had encountered some tension, Jessica swiftly moved the conversation on and suggested that they took a tour of the public rooms and some of the bedrooms. Charlotte was entranced as they walked around and she began to imagine herself in white descending the wide staircase and walking into The Orangery. Jessica wondered who, if anyone, would give the bride away, but decided not to ask. "Have you thought about flowers, especially your bouquet?" asked Jessica. "It's more of a problem in the winter. The selection of locally-grown blooms tends to be limited, and imported flowers don't last well. Some winter brides choose silk flowers."

Charlotte pulled a face. "I don't like that idea. I think artificial flowers are really tacky. I'll ask my mum. She's good at that sort of thing."

Two hours later they had unpicked a multitude of details, and Jessica had increased the couple's expenditure considerably. "Now don't forget, it's my job to make your day special. Ring me or email at any time, and I will get back to you. And let me know if you want to visit again with your mum, or anyone else for that matter. We are here to help. I'll put together a list of everything we have agreed and any outstanding points, and I'll email it to you."

"You've been so kind, thank you." Charlotte gave Jessica a hug.

Ollie put his arm round Charlotte. "I'm pleased you enjoyed this morning, but now I need to go earn some money. I think I'm going to need it."

Jessica stood in the impressive entrance and waved goodbye. "Next time bring me a photo of Joe. I can't wait to see him in his pageboy outfit!"

After they had left, Tina came to find Jessica. "That seemed to go well."

"I think it did. Have you heard from Felicity?"

"Her mum's been sent home. At first they thought it was a TIA, but it turns out the dizziness was caused by a severe ear infection. Felicity hopes to get back here before you go home."

"I'd better make sure I've got my paperwork sorted then." Jessica settled herself into the office and turned on the computer. She felt slightly unsettled by a growing suspicion. She sent a text to her father.

Dad, did you say Angie's daughter was getting married in November?
Yes, why do you ask?
Just wondered that's all. What's Angie's daughter's name?
Charlotte.

By the time Felicity returned to the hotel, Jessica had completed her paperwork ready to email. Felicity cast an eye over the details, especially the invoice total, and authorised it to be sent. "You've done very well, Jess. I am exceedingly pleased." Jessica felt proud. "No other problems?"

Jessica looked thoughtful. "No, everything seems fine."

"You'd better get off home then. You've had a long day."

Once in the car, Jessica began to think about the dilemma she had buried away in the back of her mind while talking to Felicity. Of course, she couldn't be certain that Charlotte was Angie's daughter, but it seemed highly likely. Once she knew for certain, it would be much harder to keep silent. In any case it was bound to come out before the wedding. Charlotte seemed the sort of girl who would resent the fact that Jessica had kept a secret from her. On the other hand, Charlotte had already taken against her father, so revealing the truth could completely destroy their relationship. Jessica had absolutely no idea what to do.

PART TWO

CHAPTER SEVENTEEN

The Looked-After Child

Sharon was just about to leave her office, when the duty social worker rang. "I've had a call from a Mrs Harris in Banstead Road. She's taken in Carly Collins again. Says her mum was rushed into hospital, off her head on heroin, not for the first time. That's your case, isn't it?"

Sharon put her bag down. "So much for my early night. Have we got any short-term carer places available? Carly's already on the at-risk register, so it'll have to go to court, but I doubt they'll let her return to her mum."

"You're in luck. I've got two possible spaces, Philippa Jones and Brenda Carson."

"Can you ring then and secure the placement for a couple of nights? Try Brenda first. She's a bit gentler than Philippa. I like little Carly, and she deserves a bit of kindness. We might even persuade Brenda to keep her."

"That'll be up to the courts as well, won't it?"

"Of course it will, but for now we just need a temporary order. The official court case will take time, though it's unlikely that they would want to disrupt a settled placement. Good foster carers are like gold dust, and I could see Carly settling with Brenda. See what you can do. Leave a message on my mobile."

It was getting dark when Sharon parked outside the flats in Banstead Road. She locked her car and entered the lobby. She noticed a faint smell of stale urine, and a teenage girl was leaning against the graffiti-filled wall and smoking. "You the social? Carly's in number six with Mrs Harris. Lifts are broken, you'll have to climb the stairs."

"Thank you, I've been there before."

"Poor kid," said the teenager. "Her mum was off her head on the stairs. The police chucked two blokes out of her flat and called the paras. What will happen to Carly?"

"I'm finding her a place to stay." Sharon checked her phone. There was a text from duty.

Brenda will take her.

"Nope, I've found her a place to stay," said Sharon with relief as she began to climb the stairs.

Mrs Harris had left her door open, and Sharon called out from the hallway. "It's only me. Can I come through?"

An elderly voice responded, "We're in the kitchen."

Six-year-old Carly was seated at the Formica table with a sandwich.

"Lo Sharon, Mummy's in hospital. Have you found someone to have me?"

Sharon had become used to the way that many needy children accepted their problems as normal.

"I have, Carly, a very kind lady called Brenda. Finish your sandwich, and we'll be off."

"We've packed a bag," announced Mrs Harris. She knew the drill.

"Say thank you to Mrs Harris, Carly."

"Thank you for habin' me."

"You're very welcome, Carly." The elderly lady gave the child a hug and handed her over to the social worker.

Forty minutes later, Carly was sitting on the rug in Brenda's living room building a tower with brightly-coloured pieces of giant

Lego. It was unusual for a child to be able to stay longer than a few days in an emergency placement, but Sharon's experienced judgement had been correct. Recently-widowed Brenda took to Carly. She found the child affectionate, placid, if rather too trusting. Carly was to remain in the care of her new foster mother for the next twelve years. Tantrums only ever occurred after her occasional visits to her mother. The placement was considered a success, although Brenda resented the continual scrutiny by Social Services. Brenda felt the injustice of it. *If Carly was my own child*, the foster parent reflected, *I wouldn't have to suffer this level of intrusion.*

It became easier when Carly reached sixteen, but there were still social workers in the background, asking questions about drugs, education, STDs and alcohol, so Brenda was enormously relieved when Paul appeared on the scene. He was older than Carly and seemed genuinely to care about her. Apparently, they had met in a local park, when Paul had noticed Carly sitting alone on a bench. Paul had shown an interest in the seventeen-year-old college student. He didn't seem worried by Carly's 'looked-after' status, had made a point of meeting Brenda early in the relationship, and showed respect for both Carly and Brenda. Carly would be obliged to leave her foster placement when she was eighteen, and Brenda hoped that Paul would be there to support her. Brenda, now in her mid-sixties, had sometimes wondered why Paul was quite so keen on Carly, but she was a pretty girl, and young men were easily swayed by good looks.

CHAPTER EIGHTEEN

Abuse

Carly moved in with Paul on her eighteenth birthday. The couple quickly relocated to a new address closer to the centre of Reading, and Paul advised Carly to make a fresh start by cutting all ties with her time in care. Brenda was not given Carly's address, and Paul bought Carly a new mobile phone with a new number. Carly was accustomed to having her lifestyle monitored, so Paul's detailed questioning about her movements and her choice of friends did not alarm her. She assumed his controlling manner was a normal part of a caring relationship. Although she missed Brenda, in their first year living together, Carly was not unhappy.

Paul first hit Carly when she was nineteen. She had popped out to the corner shop for some milk and stopped to chat to a friend on the way home. When she returned to the flat, Paul was waiting by the door. "Where on earth have you been?" His face was distorted with anger. She could smell alcohol.

"I stopped for a chat with Tracy."

"Didn't you realise I'd be worried about you? I tried to ring you, but your phone went to ansaphone."

"It's out of battery. I forgot to charge it."

"Do I have to remember everything for you? Milk, charging

your phone, what will you forget next? You don't forget to ask me for money every week."

"The money's for our food, Paul. You said you didn't want me to work." It was the first time Carly had dared to argue back. His response was instant. He clenched his fist and struck her hard on the side of her face. She fell to the floor, catching her forehead on the corner of the hall table. Blood began to trickle down the side of her cheek. Paul fetched a tissue and wiped her face.

His face crumpled into contrition. "I'm so sorry, darling. I didn't mean to hurt you. I was just really worried when you didn't come straight home. You're very vulnerable. You need me to help you. I must know where you are." Paul had often reminded Carly how needy she was. As soon as her wound was dressed, he kissed her repeatedly. "I have to show you how much I love you." He grasped her hand and led her to the bedroom. She was surprised at the speed with which he tugged at her jeans and lifted her top. He seemed somehow energised by his earlier violence. He left her no time to feel aroused. He pinned her arms to the bed and pushed his tongue into her throat so she could barely breathe. She felt the full weight of his body. The sex was over in minutes. "You see, I told you how much I love you. You are mine always." He left her staring at her bruised face in the mirror, while he quickly dressed and made them both a cup of tea. He brought the drink to the bedroom, stroked her hair and told her gently how beautiful she looked. Carly began to wonder if she had imagined the violence, especially as it was not repeated in the next few months. She told herself it was, at worst, an isolated incident. She needed Paul. He was right. She wouldn't cope without him.

The next time he hurt her was on her twentieth birthday. He had treated her to wine and a rare meal out. As soon as they arrived back at the flat, he changed. He looked angry, and Carly recognised the distorted face from the previous violent incident. "You really embarrassed me in that restaurant. You don't know how to behave in public, leaning over the table and encouraging the waiter to stare at your cleavage."

"I wasn't, Paul. I just wanted to look nice for you."

"Your mother was a tart, and so are you."

"That's not fair. I love you."

Paul gripped her shoulders and shook her. Once again, he punched the side of her face, but this time steadied her body to prevent a fall. He grasped her hair and pulled her into the bedroom. "You wanna behave like a whore, and I will treat you like one." He ripped the front of her new dress and violently grabbed one of her breasts. She cried out in pain. He put his other hand over her mouth. "Quiet, whore." He was unstoppable. Carly gripped the side of the bed and made no complaint. When the assault was over, he walked into the kitchen and made them both a cup of tea. He sat alongside Carly as if nothing unusual had happened. "Happy birthday, darling." The following morning, after Paul had gone to work, Carly pushed her hair over her cheek to cover the bruising on the side of her face. She winced at the pain of her breasts and thighs when she dressed. She must try harder to keep Paul happy.

The violent episodes recurred, though not frequently. Each time Carly would convince herself it would not happen again. Months would pass between attacks. She could never predict them. She continued to believe that he loved her, that she would not manage alone. She had spent her childhood in care. Her mother had been a prostitute and a drug addict. She was vulnerable. Paul had said so. He looked after her.

On her twenty-third birthday, Paul took Carly to the same restaurant where they had eaten when she was twenty. Carly was careful not to wear a low-cut top. She had learned to agree with everything Paul said. He was attentive as dinner was served, but during the meal he drank heavily, and she began to feel an undercurrent of anger. His silent aggression grew on the walk home. She felt the pain as he gripped her hand too tightly. "I saw you trying to be nice to me. I know it's an effort. You don't really love me. You just want my money." Carly made no attempt to argue with Paul. When they reached the flat, she rushed into the bedroom and barricaded the door closed with a chair. He tapped gently on the door. "Let me in, Carly."

"No, Paul, I won't."

He kicked the door violently until it flew open. The physical exertion seemed to feed his aggression. "You don't lock me out of my own bedroom. You need me, Carly." He was overwhelmed with anger, and the subsequent attack lacked his usual control. She woke the following morning with red weals across her face, severe bruising on her legs and thighs, and the pain of two broken ribs. Paul brought her tea and two paracetamol before he left for work the following day. He kissed her gently on the forehead. "I'll see you tonight."

Carly looked out of the bedroom window and watched him drive away. She managed to walk to the bathroom and then dressed in loose clothing. She entered the kitchen and peered into the housekeeping tin. It contained £85. She opened Paul's desk and rummaged through the paperwork. There was no money or birth certificates. She went back into the bedroom and searched through his jackets. She discovered a wad of notes in an inside pocket. She packed a small wheeled suitcase with some clothes, her sketch book, phone charger, a hand-sewn cloth dog and a photo of her mother. With her mobile phone and the cash in her shoulder bag, she wheeled the suitcase out of the flat and locked the door. On impulse, she posted her keys through the letterbox. She must not be tempted to return. Her determination to leave seemed to anaesthetise the pain in her ribs as she pulled the case to Reading station. She handed £50 to the man in the ticket office. "Where will this take me?"

"Where d'you want to go?"

"As far away as possible, south, somewhere remote."

The man checked his computer. "Littlehampton, £47 off-peak return."

"I don't want a return."

"£46 then, change at Gatwick. The train from Gatwick splits at Haywards Heath. Make sure you're in the right half of the train. You've got ten minutes." He printed off the journey details and gave them to Carly with her change. "Good luck!" he called after her.

CHAPTER NINETEEN

Flight

There were no vacant seats on the train to Gatwick. Carly stood in the aisle with her case between her legs. She leant against one of the seats, occasionally clutching the headrest to keep herself upright. A smartly-dressed young man leant down and lifted her case onto the overhead rack. She smiled a thank you. The paracetamol was wearing off, and she could feel a sharp pain in her ribs every time the train jumped before it slowed into a station. She felt a sense of relief as the signs for Gatwick finally appeared through the window. The man reached up to the rack and lifted down her case. Carly heard a steady bleep before the passengers began to push forward towards the opening doors. She grabbed her case and stumbled onto the platform. "There's a lift over there," the man in a suit spoke. "Where are you going?"

"Littlehampton."

"You need platform seven. The train splits at Haywards Heath." Carly followed the man to the lift. He stood against the open lift door to give her time to wheel her case inside. They remained silent while the lift ascended to the large crowded walkway. "Platform seven is down there. You'll need another lift." He watched Carly disappear into the crowd, before turning towards the exit.

The train for Littlehampton was already pulling into platform seven as Carly emerged from the second lift. She pulled her case up inside the train, just before the whistle blew and the doors closed. She lifted her case onto an empty seat and sat down beside it. She delved into her pocket and found a blister pack with two remaining paracetamol. There was a bottle of water in the front of her case, and she took a mouthful to wash down the painkillers. The pain in her ribs slowly diminished, and the rhythm of the train relaxed her body. She drifted into intermittent sleep. In her semi-conscious state, she heard the announced words at Haywards Heath, 'Make sure you are in the right part of the train', but she did not grasp their meaning. Despite the jolt as the train split in two, Carly's eyes remained closed. Her sleep deepened, as the train carried her away from Littlehampton through the East Sussex countryside towards Lewes and Eastbourne. The train finished its journey in Hastings, where Carly finally opened her eyes. The supervisor moved through the train and gently touched her shoulder. "We've arrived, miss. Time to get out."

"Am I in Littlehampton?"

"This is the Hastings part of the train. Did you want Littlehampton?"

"It doesn't matter." Carly stood up and grabbed her case. She stepped out onto the platform and slowly pulled her case past the Hastings signs towards the exit. The barriers were open, and her eyes were dazzled by the daylight as she stepped out into the open air. She scanned her environment and began to feel dizzy. A large NHS sign was looming across the road. Carly pulled her case over the pedestrian crossing and entered the walk-in medical centre. She collapsed in the foyer.

Carly woke up in a general ward at the Conquest Hospital. She noticed a double line of beds, which, as far as she could tell, were filled with elderly patients. A care assistant noticed Carly was moving. "Tea? I'll see if it's allowed." Carly tried to sit up and realised there were bandages around her ribs. She felt stiff and weak.

A nurse in dark blue uniform came and helped her. "It's Carly, isn't it? We got your name from the sketch book in your bag. Do you have a last name?"

"It's just Carly."

"Just Carly is fine. This is the Conquest Hospital. You were brought in from the walk-in medical centre in Hastings. You have extensive bruising and two broken ribs. Do you want to tell me how that happened?"

"No."

"Can I call anyone for you?"

"No."

The sister sighed inwardly. "We'll bring you tea, and we can talk again later. Are you hungry?"

"I think I am."

The sister instructed the care assistant to add a plate of toast to the order for tea. She phoned Carmel at the New Start office. "I've got one for you, hopefully, Carmel. In her early twenties, I'd guess. Broken ribs, evidence of physical and sexual abuse, but saying nothing. No surname, no family, no drugs or alcohol in her system or signs of injecting. She looks clean. She can't stay here. She's bed blocking, but if we chuck her out, then she'll certainly be at risk."

"I'll need a referral, either from Social Services or the Chaplaincy. Then someone can visit."

Sister Richards was irritated that her judgement was not considered sufficient, but she knew the system. She phoned the Chaplain's office. "I need someone to come and chat to a patient, hopefully for a referral to New Start. A woman if possible, there's suspected domestic abuse."

Shortly afterwards, a middle-aged lady approached Carly's bedside and sat down. "It's Carly, isn't it? My name is Lisa. I'm a volunteer for the hospital chaplaincy service."

"I'm not religious."

"Neither am I, Carly. I'm just here to help you. You'll soon be sent out of hospital, and I want to make sure you have somewhere to stay. Is there anyone I can call?"

"No."

"Is there somewhere you can go?"

Carly hesitated. "No."

"It's not a good idea to sleep rough with two broken ribs, Carly. Have you slept rough before?"

"No."

"Look, I can probably find you a bed, but I will need some information. Try and answer as many questions as you can. All your answers will be kept confidential. Do you understand, Carly?"

Carly nodded. "The ward sister said you don't do drugs, is that right?"

"I don't do drugs, never have."

"No alcohol problems?"

"No."

"Carly, have you been a victim of domestic abuse? I don't need details, just a yes or no."

Carly thought hard. Was she a victim of abuse? She supposed she must be. She nodded.

"Do you have past experience of the care system?"

"I'm too old to be in care. They chuck you out at eighteen."

"I just need to know if you've ever been in care, Carly. If I can tick the 'looked-after' box, it gives you priority."

"I was in care."

"Good. Well, I don't mean good about being in care, but I think you will be eligible for help. I'll need a date of birth and a surname. You can make them up if you want."

Paperwork complete, Lisa rang New Start back. "Carly Smith, date of birth 5th of 11th 1994. Looked-after status, as a minor. Now victim of domestic abuse. No evidence of illegal drugs or excessive alcohol. Two broken ribs, evidence of sexual assault, homeless. Do you have a bed?"

"She seems to fit our criteria. I'll check and call you back." The New Start officer rang back quickly.

"We've got two spaces at Orchid House. I'm free this afternoon, I'll come and have a look at her."

Lisa returned to Carly's ward. "A lady called Carmel will come and chat to you this afternoon. She can be a bit officious, so smarten yourself up and try to look grateful. It could be the difference between sleeping in a warm bed and sleeping on the pavement. Do you understand what I'm saying, Carly?"

Much to Lisa's surprise, Carly grinned. "I understand."

She stretched out her hand and winced. "Could you please pass me my bag? I want to brush my hair."

"Good girl."

Carly was interviewed by Carmel later that day, and offered a bed at Orchid House. The doctor signed her release from hospital at noon the following day.

CHAPTER TWENTY

Orchid House

Carly wearily bumped her suitcase along the uneven paving which led to Orchid House. It had taken her over an hour to walk from the Conquest Hospital to the road which housed the charity hostel. She was still clutching the £6 taxi money, donated by New Start, but which she had decided to save by walking. She rang the bell and announced her name. "Come on up." The door clicked open. A short flight of stairs led to an office with a glass-fronted window. A young woman came out to greet her. "You must be Carly. You look tired. Sit down and I'll fetch you a cup of tea." The young woman returned with a china mug. "Be careful, it's hot. I'm afraid the tea in the canteen comes out lukewarm in paper cups, so make the most of this one." She watched Carly as she sipped the tea. "Two broken ribs, isn't it?" Carly nodded. "I'll give you a couple of paracetamol to get you through. Don't tell anyone. They're very strict about tablets here. If you want any more, you'll have to sign for them."

"Thank you."

"Are you well enough to listen for a few minutes?"

"I'm fine."

"Hmmm… you don't look fine. I'm Kirsty, Orchid House admin and general dogsbody. You'll meet Frances, the boss, after breakfast tomorrow. In the meantime, I need to fill you in on some stuff. Orchid House is owned and run by New Start, a charity for young women who have fallen on hard times. We give priority to care leavers and victims of domestic abuse. Places are always in demand, and the rules are very strict. No drugs, alcohol, swearing, stealing or violent behaviour is allowed. There's a rota for cooking and cleaning. There are no second chances. Break the rules, and we kick you out. If you self-harm, you must report it, and we expect everyone to attend all group meetings and assigned workshop sessions. You'll get help with your CV. We aim to find you employment and your own shared accommodation within six months. Understand?"

"Yes."

"I'm putting you in a room with Donna on the third floor. She knows the ropes, but has nearly been thrown out twice, so don't be led astray by her. Bring your case and follow me." Carly just about managed to lift her case up the three flights of stairs and entered her new room. It was painted in cream with bottle green woodwork. There was one small wardrobe, a wooden chair, and two beds, each beside a chest of drawers. The windows appeared to be barricaded shut by large horizontal pieces of wood which were screwed to the wall. Kirsty opened the wardrobe door and sighed at the mess. "You'll have to ask Donna to make room for you. Breakfast is at 8 am. Arrive late, and you'll miss it. Have you got an alarm?"

"Yes, on my phone."

"Set it then, and keep your phone close. They tend to walk in this place. Donna will be back soon. The bathroom is on the floor below."

Finally alone, Carly sat on the bed beside the empty drawers and examined her surroundings. Despite the bleak décor, and basic furnishing, she felt safe. She lay on the bed and fell quickly asleep. She awoke an hour later, aware of a hand in her bag. "Hi there, I'm Donna." Donna moved quickly to her own bed.

Carly grabbed her bag and closed it. "Did you take anything?"

"Don't be daft. I was just being nosy." Carly felt uneasy and glanced inside her bag.

"You see, it's all still in there. Do you want help unpacking?"

"I can manage, thank you." Carly lifted her suitcase onto the bed, then sat down in pain. "Sorry, I have broken ribs. They still hurt a bit."

"Bloody bully. I hope he doesn't live round here. Have you got painkillers?" Carly nodded. Donna continued, "If you don't need the painkillers, keep them safe. You might be able to swap them for something." She talked incessantly while Carly slowly unpacked her suitcase and placed each item in the chest of drawers. "You haven't got much, have you? Still that's good, because I've got loads and need the space." Carly finally removed the hand-sewn cloth dog and sat him on the chest of drawers. Donna picked it up and examined it. "This is cute. A present from the bully?"

"No, I made it… when I was thirteen."

"What, all by yourself?" Carly nodded.

"Could you make me one?" asked Donna.

"Probably." Carly instinctively realised it was in her interests to be useful to Donna. "I'll need a needle and thread."

"They'll give you a sewing kit downstairs. They run workshops on sewing. 'Make do and mend', they call it. I call it boring."

"I'll see what I can do then." Carly suddenly felt hungry. She took a banana from her bag which she had saved from the hospital.

"Is that all you've got? They'll give you food vouchers tomorrow, but they don't buy much, so you need to fill up on breakfast. Breakfast is free. There's a water machine on the landing and a microwave, toaster and vending machine in the canteen. They don't trust us with a kettle."

"I'm not that hungry, the banana is fine." Carly went onto the landing and filled a plastic cup with water. She returned and took the paracetamol.

"There's a TV room downstairs if you like soaps. Gets a bit mouthy though."

"How many here?"

"Twenty-two when it's full, but people come and go. You want to watch TV?"

"Maybe tomorrow. I'm really tired." Donna disappeared downstairs.

Carly approached the larger window and scanned the view. She could see a hillside with a castle and the sea beyond. There seemed to be rows of tall, terraced houses, and possibly some shops. She opened the tourist map of Hastings which Carmel had given her. Orchid House was marked by a pencil arrow in one corner, and Carly tried to link the view from the window with landmarks on the map. She found the castle and began to make sense of her surroundings. She then removed her trousers and jacket, and climbed into bed, partially clothed, with her bag beside her under the sheets. She propped herself up on the pillow and found a pen and her sketchbook. She began to write a list. By the time Donna returned to the room at the curfew time of 10.30 pm, Carly was fast asleep.

The alarm rang at 7.15 am. Carly had switched on her phone for the first time since leaving Reading, but set it to airplane mode. She had no future plans except that she didn't want to be discovered and had added the words 'change phone number' to her list. Donna was already dressed, and playing loud music from a small radio. Carly could hear footsteps and female screams from the room above. Donna shouted towards the ceiling, "Shut up!" It made no difference. She watched Carly select clean underwear from her drawer. "I've got some washing powder if you need it. Or there's a laundry room downstairs."

"Thanks, I might rinse a couple of bits later, if the bathroom's free."

"Time to fill up," yelled a voice from the landing, and Carly and Donna headed towards the canteen. The room was full of scantily-dressed young women, who all seemed to understand the routine. Carly stood back and watched, while Donna pushed into a queue. A voice beside her spoke, "You new? I'll help you. Drinks are over there, and you have to make your own toast. There's also cornflakes and milk. Get what you want, and I'll watch your plate for you, while you fetch a drink."

"What about yours?"

"I've got my drink. You can watch it, when I get my toast."

"Thank you." Carly queued for the toast machine and put two slices on a plate with some margarine and a spoonful of marmalade. She returned and sat next to her new companion.

"Go get a drink, then it's my turn."

Carly approached an older lady who was pouring weak, milky tea into paper cups. "Tea please," requested Carly.

"Certainly, madam. It's nice to serve a polite one for a change." Carly hoped no one had heard and returned to her seat. Her companion immediately left her chair and returned with toast and cereal. She looked at Carly. "You're sharing with Donna, aren't you?"

"Yes."

"Nice of her to look after you!"

"I think she was hungry."

"Watch your stuff, she's light-fingered." Carly examined her new friend. She spoke with an educated accent like Paul's and didn't really seem to fit in.

"I know what you're thinking. I'm too posh for a hostel. Abuse is not selective." Carly wasn't sure she understood, so said nothing. "This place is a bit Dickensian, one step up from the poorhouse. They make us suffer for our misfortune. Apparently weak tea is good for the soul. But it's a stepping stone, if you make use of it."

Carly smiled. "Thanks for your help."

"You're welcome. No one helped me when I first came. You look pale. You okay?"

"Broken ribs."

"And a broken heart no doubt. I'm Camilla, bloody stupid name for an abused posh girl." She held out her hand to Carly.

"I'll check the rota for you." Camilla walked to the notice board and read a large chart. "No domestic duties for you today. Broken ribs obviously get you a reprieve, but you're down for tomorrow, and you have a meeting today with Frances in the office at 10.30. Be humble. She thinks I'm arrogant. And listen carefully. She only says things once. You want cereal? They'll close the canteen soon."

"I couldn't."

"You must eat. A full stomach will help to mend an empty soul." Carly looked confused.

"Just do your best to eat. I'm in room three if you need anything."

"Thank you."

Promptly at 10.30 am, Carly knocked on the office door. She could see Frances through the glass.

"Enter." Carly walked into the office, and Frances pointed to a chair. She sat down ready to listen.

"I know Kirsty went over the rules with you yesterday, but I'm going to repeat them. Basically, we are entirely funded by donations, so we don't have time for slackers or time wasters. Stick to the rules, and we'll provide an address for benefits and prepare you for employment. Break the rules, and we kick you out." Frances reiterated the rules which Kirsty had explained the day before, but added some details about paperwork and security. "I don't need your real name. We can designate you as 'at risk' and set you up with a new National Insurance Number. You must attend the compulsory counselling sessions though. Now what work experience do you have?"

"None."

"Not even a holiday job?"

"No, nothing."

"What about school work placements?"

"Looked afters were sent on a care leavers course instead."

"Well what can you do? Computers?"

"A bit." Carly thought. "I've got A-levels, but I don't have the certificates any more. I can sew really well and mend things. I was told to ask for a sewing kit."

"Do you have something to mend?"

"Yes," Carly lied.

"That's good, money-saving." Frances produced a small cardboard sewing kit from a drawer. She also gave Carly an envelope which contained £20 worth of food vouchers and a list of participating supermarkets. Carly was instructed to sign for the vouchers. She wrote 'Carly Smith'. Interview over, Carly returned to her room clutching the vouchers and the small sewing kit.

She put the food vouchers and tourist map in her home-made cloth bag and, for the first time since her arrival at Orchid House, stepped out into the fresh air. It was nearly midday, and the bright sunshine made her feel giddy. She followed the roads down towards the coast until she came across a street with run-down shops which appeared to lead into town. She wandered into an old-fashioned specialist sewing shop and glanced despondently at the prices of fabric and sewing machines. A little further down was a large kiosk full of phone cases and second-hand phones. The sign said 'PHONES UNLOCKED'. Carly entered. She removed her phone from her bag and showed the shopkeeper. "I need to change my number, but I don't have much money." Carly handed over the upgraded phone which Paul had given her as recompense after one of his outbursts. It was in her name, and pay as you go, but he had never given her enough money to keep it topped up.

"Is that on contract, or do you own it?"

"It's mine, on pay as you go."

"It's a good phone. I could swap it for a cheaper one, change the number, and throw in some credit?"

"What will happen to the old number?"

"Once I destroy the SIM card, it will come up as unobtainable."

Carly got the impression he had done this before. "What phone will you give me?"

He rummaged under the counter. "This one. It's only a couple of years old with a great camera, but it's cheap because it's not a trendy make. You give me your phone, and I'll give you this one with a new SIM card, £30 credit and 500 free texts."

Carly thought quickly. "How about £40 credit?"

"£35."

"Done," agreed Carly.

"I'll throw in a free case," offered the shopkeeper, "but I'll need a name for the old phone for my records. I don't want to be accused of accepting stolen goods."

"Carly Smith." A few minutes later, Carly was walking down the road clutching her new phone in its bright blue case. She wanted to ring someone, anyone, but there was no one to ring.

Her next stop was the supermarket. She had £20 worth of food vouchers to last her a week. Carly wandered around the aisles checking prices. She went outside and sat on a bench to make yet another list. *Bread, cheap spread, cuppa soup, jam.* "Nothing to go in the fridge," Camilla had advised. "People will pinch it."

"I ought to get something healthy," Carly spoke out loud. She wrote the words *Look at fruit* then decided to shop for food on her return journey. As she headed further into town, Carly started to search for charity shops. She entered each one and began to glance around. Whilst other potential customers examined the clothing for style and size, Carly sought out fabrics which could be cut up and transformed into animal shapes. She rummaged through the 50p box and pulled out two paisley scarves of different colours. "Perfect." She handed the assistant £1. The assistant noticed the fading marks on Carly's face.

"Have them both for 50p." Carly didn't argue.

Lunchtime was approaching, and Carly began to feel weary. Her ribs were hurting, and she could smell burgers cooking from an outdoor food outlet. She sat down at a bus stop and counted the money in her wallet. She resisted the burgers and walked back to the supermarket. With a cheap bag of apples added to her shopping and 5p cash required for a plastic bag, Carly finally spent one £5 food voucher then slowly headed back to Orchid House. They buzzed her in. The house was very peaceful, and she climbed up the stairs to her room. There was a blunt knife in the adjacent kitchenette, which she used to make a jam sandwich. She filled her water bottle and settled on the bed with her lunch. The food made her tired, and once again she drifted into sleep. When Carly awoke it was mid-afternoon.

Orchid House was still very quiet, and Carly wondered where everyone was. Frances had explained that all residents had to attend regular workshops and go for job interviews, so maybe that was where they all were. She tried to bend and reach down to the sewing kit in the bottom drawer, but her body would not co-operate. She climbed off the bed and knelt down. The sewing kit contained several colours of thread, two buttons, a few pins, a needle, and a tiny pair of scissors. Carly noticed an old magazine under the bed and picked it up. She began to draw the outline of a rabbit on one of the pages. Once satisfied, she used the little scissors to cut out the template. She carefully pinned the paper shape to one of the scarves, which she had folded in half. Despite the size of the scissors, within ten minutes Carly had produced two identical paisley rabbit bodies, ready to hand sew together. She cut out the ear shapes and used a small part of the other scarf to prepare linings for the ears and to add a round nose to the face.

Donna suddenly burst in carrying two bags of shopping. She bounced on the end of Carly's bed, and made her wince. "Wow, Carly, you're making a rabbit. Is that for me?"

"If you want."

"Oh, yes please." The 'please' made Carly smile. It was the first time Donna had been polite.

"I've still got to sew it together and do the eyes and whiskers. And I'll need something to stuff it with."

"Like cotton wool?"

"That sort of thing."

Donna rummaged through her wardrobe and produced a pack of cotton wool balls.

"Will this do?"

"Don't you need them?"

"I'll get some more." Carly wondered where Donna got her money from. "Can I name the rabbit now, before it's finished?"

"If you like."

"I'll call her Tania, after my mum."

"Tania, it is then." Carly carefully double-stitched the sides of the rabbit, suspecting that Donna might be a bit rough with her new paisley friend. "You don't mind that it's not a dog?"

"It's cool." Donna watched as Carly crammed the cotton wool into the cloth animal until its body was plump, and the material tightly stretched around its base and tummy. She gripped the neck opening as she pushed the last of the cotton wool into the rabbit's head, and sewed up the opening.

"I have to leave it to settle now. I'll add the face and ears later." Carly put the unfinished rabbit into her bag.

The days at Orchid House stretched into weeks. The marks on Carly's face began to fade, and the pain in her ribs subsided. She quickly adjusted to the domestic routine and was helped to complete the paperwork to apply for benefits. Despite the limits of the food vouchers, she began to put on weight. Each morning, after her chores, she would walk into town and wander around the charity shops, occasionally buying an inexpensive dress or scarf, which she could recycle into a soft toy or cloth bag. The staff at Orchid House were impressed with her efforts and allowed her to borrow some sharp scissors, as long as she handed them in each evening to be locked away. Towards the end of each day she would sit on Camilla's bed and chat while she stitched. "You like making those animals, don't you? They're very good."

"Donna likes hers."

"She needs something to give her unconditional love. Every bloke she's ever met has wanted something back. I'm convinced she's dealing drugs. She always seems to have money. Carly, you do realise they'll stop your food vouchers, when you get your benefits?"

"I thought they would. I've got a mock job interview next week. I'm a bit scared."

"You'll be fine. You're brighter than most of the girls here. Anyway, it's just practice, and a few days before the interview, you get £30 to buy something smart."

"You're joking!"

"Nope, it'll really happen, but you have to keep the receipts and give back any change."

"I won't know what to buy."

"I'll come with you if you like, be like a girls' shopping trip." Sure enough, three days before Carly's interview, she noticed a meeting with Frances had appeared on her work rota. At exactly the correct time, Carly tapped on the office door.

"Enter." Carly was now familiar with this command. "Take a seat." There followed a list of instructions about suitable interview clothing, spending money wisely, and keeping receipts. Frances made it abundantly clear that she did not believe the girls should be given this one-off clothing allowance, but she had been over-ruled by the trustees. Eventually, after the usual 'Frances lecture' (which is how Camilla had described it), Carly was invited to sign for the envelope of thirty pounds in cash. She headed straight to Camilla's room and knocked on the door, before entering. "Got it!" Carly waved the envelope at Camilla, who grabbed the new cloth shoulder bag which Carly had recently finished for her.

"Let's go then!"

The two girls walked quickly into the town centre and sat on a bench near the central market. "Look that stall's got loads of bags like the ones you make, Carly. I wonder how much they are?"

Camilla walked over to the stall, lifted up one of the bags and spoke to the trader. "How much are these?"

"The large ones are £5.99. I like yours, where did you get it?"

"My friend makes them. Would you be interested in buying a few?"

The stallholder paused and examined Camilla's bag. "This is hand-stitched. I would need them done by machine. Your friend got a sewing machine, has she?"

"Oh, yes," lied Camilla. "She just did mine by hand, as a one-off."

"Tell your friend, I could take twenty-five machine-stitched ones, on a trial basis, at £2 each. They'd have to be good quality though, and I'd want them by the end of next week, before I re-stock."

"That's a deal then," agreed Camilla, and she shared the news with Carly.

"How am I going to get hold of a sewing machine and enough material for twenty-five bags?" asked Carly.

"You'll find a way. You always do. This is a great opportunity."

The two girls headed to the department store. It was 'Blue Cross' day, and Carly managed to buy a black suit and shoes for just under £20. Carly didn't really want black, but Camilla insisted. "It's what they'll expect at Orchid, and it does suit you. You look really pretty, now you've put some weight on. Shame we can't afford a decent haircut, but if you borrow the scissors, you could ask Chelsea to have a go at your hair when we get back. She's good at cutting hair."

Carly looked thoughtful. "I will, but I'm not sure why I'm bothering. I don't ever want another man in my life." Camilla decided not to argue with her friend. Carly needed a top to wear under the suit, so they began to rummage in one of the charity shops. A suitable white top was found, and Carly began to search through boxes of patterned curtains. She picked up a selection and showed Camilla. These would make brilliant bags. I could even use the lining. The material is really strong, and they've all been cleaned."

"I said you were resourceful. Bring what you want and come with me." Camilla spoke to the lady behind the desk. "If we bought this white top and three pairs of curtains, could you put it all on the receipt for the white top?"

"Don't see why not. It'll be £7 though. Seems a lot for one top."

"You okay with that, Carly?" asked Camilla.

"Why not?" The deal was done.

On their return, Carly folded the curtains into a plastic bag under her bed and hung her outfit on one of the wooden batons protecting the bedroom window. Donna had never cleared any space for Carly in the wardrobe, but at least Carly could be confident Donna would not want to borrow her new outfit. It was far too conventional. Carly then went down to the office and handed in the envelope with £3.51 change and the receipts. Donna was sitting in the bedroom when Carly returned. "That outfit is gross! I bet Camilla chose it. You should've taken me." Carly was aware that Donna was growing increasingly envious of her friendship with Camilla. Later that evening, she took her phone down to Camilla's room.

"I need to ask you something."

"Of course. I like to be useful. What's up?"

"I'm worried about Donna. She's turning nasty. Can I put my number on your phone in case I need your help in an emergency? But you must keep the number secret." Carly sent Camilla one of her free texts, and Camilla replied.

CHAPTER TWENTY-ONE

The Private Detective

Neil approached the counter at the station café. He showed the waitress a photo of Carly. "I just wondered if you recognised this young woman? I'm trying to trace her."

"She in trouble?"

"Not as far as I know. This is a missing person investigation on behalf of family."

"Maybe she wants to be missing."

"Maybe she does. It's just a general enquiry."

"Well I've not seen her anyway."

"May I look?" A young man in a suit stood up and looked over Neil's shoulder. Neil handed him the photo. The young man carried the photo over to the light and examined it. "I think that's the girl I saw on the Gatwick train a few weeks ago. She was very pale, and her face was scratched. I lifted her case onto the rack."

"You got time for a coffee?" asked Neil. The man in the suit nodded, and Neil brought over two Americanos in disposable cups. He placed one of the drinks in front of the young man and pulled out a second photo from the inside of his jacket. "Was this her?"

The man examined the photo. "Yes, I think so. A girl with a pale face, nervous, eyes everywhere, like a rabbit under headlights. There were red marks on her face. She was pretty, long brown hair, skinny, but nice figure, I wanted to help her. I lifted her case onto the overhead rack for her, then down again at Gatwick. We caught the lift together to the walkway, then she read the train times, grabbed her case and rushed to platform seven. I think she caught the Littlehampton train. I never saw her again, though I kept looking."

"Did she talk to you on the train to Gatwick?"

"Not a word, just stared out of the window. Is she in trouble?"

"Not as far as I know. I'm simply trying to trace her. This is my card in case you see her again or remember anything else." Neil left his full coffee cup on the table and walked back to the station concourse. He chatted to the ticket office attendant, picked up the Litttlehampton timetable, and returned to his office.

A few days later Neil contacted a former colleague from the police. Bob was pleased to accept the invitation to meet up for a coffee in Reading, though as a serving officer, he couldn't help but suspect Neil's motives. Neil carried two lattes over to the table in the café where they had agreed to meet. "Cheers." Neil lifted the cup to his mouth. Bob sat and watched him. "How's Janice?" Neil finally enquired.

"As ever, bit of arthritis, but otherwise okay."

"And the boys?"

"Men, you mean, Tim's almost thirty." Bob began to tap on the table. "What do you want, Neil? I bet you haven't brought me here to talk about Janice."

Neil grinned. "Well, I was hoping for a bit of information, and before you say no, let me explain." Neil was now retired from the police and no longer had access to police records. "I have a case, a bloke in his early thirties has asked me to trace his missing girlfriend."

"And?"

"I think I've tracked her down, living in a hostel on the south coast."

"So what d'you need me for?"

"There's something about him I don't trust. He keeps telling me how vulnerable she is, and she's now in a hostel for abused women."

"So just say you can't find her."

"And then I'd lose my fee, and he's a good payer. Also, I might be wrong about him."

"What do you want from me?"

"Just a background check, see if anything dodgy pops up." Neil handed Bob a piece of paper.

"I can't promise."

"Thanks, mate."

Neil knew Bob would do his best. It was the first time since his retirement that he had asked for Bob's help, and Bob owed him a favour. Neil had chatted to the man in the ticket office, who had remembered the girl. He recalled that she had appeared to be running away. Neil had telephoned all the hostels and cheap B and Bs in Littlehampton without success. He had then caught the identical train to Gatwick and realised the train divided at Haywards Heath. He travelled back to his office and looked at the rail map. He instinctively guessed that this girl would aim for the sea. He began to phone hostels in Brighton, Eastbourne and finally Hastings. "Could I speak to Carly Collins?" Neil had asked again and again. He had finally spoken to an inexperienced volunteer at Orchid House. "Is Carly there?"

"Which Carly?"

"Carly Collins, but she may have changed her name. She would have arrived from Reading in the past few weeks, long brown hair."

"Hang on, I'll check if she's in her room."

Neil heard raised voices in the background. A different voice came on the phone. It was Frances.

"Sorry we can't give out any information."

"So you do have a Carly?"

"And who are you to ask?"

"I'm a private detective working on behalf of a family member."

"We are a charity hostel working with vulnerable young women. We do not give out any personal information." Frances cut off the call. It was at that point that Neil had contacted Bob.

The evening after their meeting, Bob rang Neil. "Paul William Maynard. No convictions, but his name appears twice on our records six years ago for alleged domestic violence. Nothing since. Looks like your instincts could be right. I'm surprised he gave you his real name."

"I won't take on clients unless they provide ID. I've been caught out before. Thanks Neil, looks like I'll have to forfeit my finder's fee." It was a short phone call. Neil was tempted to pay Hastings a visit to confirm his theory, but experience told him to leave the investigation well alone. As far as he was concerned the case was now closed.

CHAPTER TWENTY-TWO

Homeless

The following afternoon, Frances called Carly into the office. "Sit down, Carly."

"Have I done something wrong?"

"Far from it, we're very pleased with you." Frances took a deep breath. "You mustn't let what I'm about to say worry you, Carly, but we've had an enquiry from a private detective about a Carly Collins who used to live in Reading. I'm assuming that might be you?" Carly remained silent.

"I thought so," continued Frances. "I assume you don't want us to give out any information."

Carly nodded and began to shake. "I don't want anyone to know I'm here."

"We are very discreet, Carly. He won't find out."

"He's clever. He'll come after me."

"He doesn't know where you are, Carly. You're safe here."

Nevertheless, Carly felt anxious as she returned to her room. She looked around in surprise. Donna's belongings had been unexpectedly tidied, and the room seemed unusually neat. Donna was sitting on the chair. "There was a room search while you were with Frances, looking for crack. They didn't find any."

"They didn't find any, because we don't have any... do we?"

Donna opened Carly's bottom drawer, and pulled out the toy dog. She opened the stitching underneath and removed a small white packet. "I knew they wouldn't search your stuff. So I hid it in here. It's me they were after."

Carly went white. "You could've got me chucked out."

"Don't be a wimp. They didn't find it." Donna put the drugs in her pocket and left the room.

Carly lay on her bed and said nothing. She could feel her heart pulsating in her head. All the feelings of security which had built up over the past few weeks had disappeared. She was overwhelmed with panic and felt scared and vulnerable. As soon as she was sure Donna had gone, Carly started to pack her belongings into her case, including the plastic bag which contained the curtains. She quickly folded the interview suit and made sure she had the extra cash from her benefits, which she had, for the first time, taken out of the bank the previous day. She grabbed her phone and remaining food vouchers, and crept down the stairs past the office, case in hand. Once out of the building, Carly walked swiftly to Hastings station. A sense of nostalgia briefly invaded her thoughts as she glanced at the medical centre before walking through the open barrier. Without even glancing at the illuminated timetable, Carly climbed onto a train, which pulled away within seconds.

The first stop was 'St Leonards, Warrior Square'. Three youths in hooded tops were sitting on a station bench, sharing a cigarette. Carly decided to stay on the train. The next stop said 'Bexhill on Sea'. The long platform looked clean, and two elderly ladies were stood waiting. She picked up her case and stepped off the train. A long slope led to the open barriers, and Carly walked outside. The sun was beginning to set, and she stared down the road towards the sea and a rose striped sky. A direction sign close by pointed north to Manor Gardens. Carly turned her back to the sea and began to climb the hill. She negotiated the steep pathway, crossing the road to find more pavement. Ten minutes later she found herself sitting on a bench in Manor Gardens. She pulled out her phone and texted Camilla.

Sorry I didn't say goodbye. Please don't give Orchid House my number.

The reply came quickly. *You know your secret is safe with me. What's happened?*

Paul knows where I am, and Donna planted crack on me.

Shit. Say if I can help.

Darkness was falling, and the necessity of a night sleeping rough began to turn into reality. It was a warm evening, but Carly needed to find somewhere to hide. She started to explore the gardens. A large historic barn was situated in the centre of the park. All the doors were locked, and she could see a small kitchen area through one of the windows. Behind the barn were public toilets, now closed for the night. Down a few steps beside the toilets was a large covered area with a cobbled wall on one side. Carly spread out her coat in the far corner. She lay her head on her suitcase and clutched her bag on her tummy. This, she decided, would be her resting place until morning. Sleep came quickly, but was soon interrupted. The surrounding trees began to rustle with the noise of wildlife. An owl let out the occasional menacing screech. At some point a fox crept into the barn and stared at Carly with illuminated eyes. He rushed away when Carly suddenly sat up. Carly was relieved when faint traces of morning light finally began to appear on the wood and stonework which surrounded her. She felt entirely alone.

She heard a car drive into the car park and a door slam. Footsteps walked towards the toilets, and a door was unlocked. Carly stood up and brushed herself down. She listened. Two other voices spoke. "Morning, John."

"Morning, ladies, you're early."

"Gotta 'do' this morning for Bill French's funeral. Some are coming a long way so we're serving bacon rolls and coffee before the service. We've been told to expect the first mourners by nine."

"What time's the service?"

"10 am, then a family-only burial, while the rest come back here. It's a big 'do'."

"I'll let you get on then. I'm trying to clear the summer pruning this week, and it's too hot to do it later." Carly looked at her phone. It said 7.30 am. She tried to look confident and walked to the toilet with her suitcase and bag. "Morning," said John the gardener, as she passed. "Looks like another hot day."

"It does," replied Carly. She couldn't escape from the thought of bacon rolls. She locked herself into a toilet cubicle and opened her case. The black interview suit with white top was still neatly folded on top of her other clothes. "Not too creased," she said to herself, as she changed into the brand new outfit. She stayed locked in the toilet until 8.30 am. As she stepped outside, she could smell bacon from the kitchen. She realised she had not eaten since yesterday lunchtime, and her stomach began to rumble. She rested on a bench and watched. The first cars drove into the car park just before nine and people in dark suits began to walk into the building. An older lady spotted Carly and walked over to her. "You don't have to wait outside, y'know. They're serving food before the service. Bill's family thought of everything. You family or friend?"

"Friend."

"Did you drive down today?"

"No. I came by train."

"You had an early start then. Come on, you stay with me. I'm Freda, Bill's late wife's younger sister. I'll look after you." Freda took Carly's arm and led her into the building. "Leave your case over there. It'll be quite safe." She handed Carly a plate and pointed to the bacon rolls. "I'd take two, if I were you. There seems to be plenty." Carly did as she was told and tried not to look too hungry, as she took bites of her breakfast. No one questioned her presence, as Freda introduced her to the growing number of mourners. "This is Carly, a friend of Bill's." Freda turned to Carly. "Do you recognise anyone?"

"I don't think I do."

"Well he kept you quiet, not that I'm suggesting anything, but he did like young women. Led my sister a right dance."

"I'd rather not talk about it." Carly surprised herself with the quickness of her answer.

"Quite right too. We don't want to go spreading gossip before Bill's in his grave, even if he was a bit of a bastard." Carly looked shocked.

"Sorry," apologised Freda, "that was uncalled for." Just after half-past nine, the room began to empty as people dispersed towards the church. Carly joined Freda in the short walk up the hill. Little groups had gathered around the gravestones, not wanting to enter the church too early. Eventually Freda approached Carly, and asked, "You coming in?"

"I think I'll stand at the back."

"See you later then." Freda hesitated, then turned back. "You want my tissues? I doubt that I'll need them."

"Yes, thank you."

The congregation stood as the coffin was carried towards the altar. The service lasted half an hour, during which Carly learned a lot about the provider of her bacon rolls. She got the impression that tributes were delivered with respect rather than love. When the mourners re-entered the building, the bacon rolls had been replaced with large platters of sandwiches. Most people queued for tea and coffee before approaching the food. Carly stared at the spread, and Freda spotted her. "I doubt this will all go. You've got a long journey home, you could take some with you."

"I don't like to."

"Nonsense! No one will even notice."

Carly hesitated. "I didn't intend to stay and meet the close family."

"Wise choice. That's why I'm here, and not at the burial." Freda took a carrier from her handbag and gave it to Carly. "Go on, take some. I'll stand in front of you." Carly took several sandwiches from each of the platters closest to her and slipped them into the carrier. "Nicely done," whispered Freda.

"I think I'd better go now," said Carly.

"Enjoy your tea!"

Once outside, Carly put the carrier into her suitcase and wheeled it downhill towards the seafront.

With bacon rolls in her stomach and sandwiches in her suitcase, Carly's mood lifted. She sat on a bench and enjoyed the warmth of the sun. She had a good amount of cash, and there was quite a bit more in her bank account, which was intended to go back to Orchid House for her future rent, and, of course, there was the promise of payment from the market.

CHAPTER TWENTY-THREE

The Guest House

Carly began to walk along the seafront. It was a warm morning, and people seemed happy. She tried to soak up the atmosphere. Across the road a dark-haired lady was wiping tables outside a café and talking to herself in Italian. The café was called 'That's Amore'. Carly couldn't help but reflect on how unromantic her own life had been. She walked into the De La Warr Pavilion and wandered around the shop. A young girl was sitting behind the counter. "Excuse me, is there a tourist office nearby?"

"I'm afraid not, well not one where you can speak to a real person, anyway, just a computer in a café. We don't have a manned tourist office in Bexhill. What are you looking for?"

"Somewhere to stay."

"It's pretty busy at this time of year, but you might strike lucky." The assistant stepped out from behind the counter and pointed through the glass entrance doors. "If I were you, I'd cross the road and explore the side roads. There are loads of B and Bs. Go in and ask. They sometimes get cancellations. You might strike lucky." Carly thanked her and crossed the road. She began to zigzag up and down the roads which led away from the sea. In the first road she counted five guest houses, all of which displayed a 'no vacancies' sign.

Carly finally turned into another side road and spotted a hand in the window of the Buenos Aires Guest House. The hand turned the sign from 'No Vacancies' to 'Vacancies'. Carly approached the large porch and pushed open the front door. There was a small plaque on a table in the entrance inscribed with the words 'May this house to every guest be a place of peace and rest'. She heard a voice. "I knew I should have taken a deposit. That's five days in high season we've lost." The lady opened the inner door and spotted Carly. "Can I help you?"

"I wondered how much a single room would be?" The lady looked at Carly in approval. She noted the smart suit and small suitcase.

"I don't have a single room, I'm afraid, but I've just been let down at the last minute by a couple with one child. If you take all five days, you can have their family room for a single price. I'm afraid you'll have to share a bathroom, but there is a sink in the room, and it's a good size." The lady circled the single room price on the tariff list. "That includes breakfast."

Carly did a quick calculation in her head. "I'll take it."

The lady picked up Carly's case and carried it up to the first floor. She opened a door to reveal a large traditionally-furnished spacious bedroom with a wide bay window. The room was filled with natural light, and Carly could just glimpse the sea between the surrounding buildings. "This is lovely," exclaimed Carly. She tried not to look too relieved.

"I'm Rachel," said the lady. "I run this guest house with my husband, Andy. You look a bit pale, do you need anything?"

Carly thought quickly. "No, I'm fine now. I was supposed to be staying with a friend, but she's not well. I was worried I wouldn't find anywhere."

"Well, it's lucky we had a cancellation then. Can I get you anything else?"

"Just one question," ventured Carly "Do you know where I might purchase a second-hand sewing machine? I've got a bit of time to kill, and I thought I might make my friend a bag, like this one."

Rachel looked at Carly's cloth bag. "That's lovely. Did you make it?"

Carly nodded, and Rachel continued, "You don't need to buy a machine. I'll lend you mine, if it's good enough. I haven't used it for years. Just don't sew too late at night, as it's a bit noisy. It might disturb the other guests. I'll get Andy to bring it up." Rachel left Carly alone.

Carly walked around the room and examined every detail. There was a double and a single bed and a settee with plenty of storage including an empty wardrobe with hangers. A small tray housed tea, coffee, and little cartons of milk. There was even a dressing gown to be used when visiting the shared bathroom. She suddenly felt exhausted. Carly lay on the bed and fell into a deep sleep. Some time later, she was woken by a loud knock. Andy slowly opened the door and peered in. Carly stood up. "One sewing machine, young lady." He picked it up from the landing floor. "Where shall I put it?"

Carly hesitated. "How about here?"

Andy placed the sewing machine on one of the chests of drawers. "You're lucky to have this room. It's normally reserved for families. You'll have plenty of light while you're sewing."

"Thank you. It's perfect." Andy went back outside and returned with an old-fashioned wicker sewing basket and an extension lead.

"Sorry there's no instructions for the machine, but I'm sure you'll work it out. Rachel thought you might need a few things, so she said to help yourself from her basket. It used to belong to her Mum."

"Thank you, that is so kind." When Andy had left, Carly opened the basket and examined its contents. As well as a selection of thread, pins and needles, there were zips and ribbons, and pieces of lace, mixed with cardboard strips of fasteners and little tins of buttons. Carly delved through the basket like a child who had been given a large box of candy. She pulled out a heavy pair of scissors and put them on the chest of drawers beside her bed. She opened her case and removed the curtains. Four pairs were placed neatly in a drawer, and she laid one curtain on the floor. Using her own bag as a template, she began to calculate how many bags she could make from one curtain. Carly was accustomed to being economical. Paul had always kept her short of money, and she had learned not to waste anything. She was also in the habit of hiding away things which she enjoyed, in case Paul removed them as a punishment. She unpacked her clothes from the case, and then put the roughly-pinned curtain back in the drawer. She instinctively knew that she should not leave evidence of her sewing enterprise on view in her bedroom. She finally slipped her phone, food vouchers and a carrier bag back into her shoulder bag, locked the bedroom door and went downstairs.

Carly began to retrace her steps towards Bexhill station. The De La Warr Pavilion dominated the first part of the seafront, but after that she noticed more cafés close to the sea and streets of shops which seemed to lead north. By following the directions to Manor Gardens, she rediscovered the station. She went into the station lobby and picked up a free magazine, then peered into the waiting room and spotted a local newspaper which had been discarded. Another sign directed her to a local supermarket, which was her next stop. She used one of her remaining food vouchers to buy noodles, biscuits and soup. She didn't want to appear poor, so knew she would have to be discreet. Armed with her papers and purchases, Carly took a different route through the town centre and found her way back to the guest house. She treated herself to a cup of tea, a biscuit and the last of the sandwiches and spent the evening working on the newspaper templates for the twenty-five cloth bags which she was planning to create. When her eyes became too tired to work, Carly played with the remote control for the television. Neither Paul nor the residents at Orchid House had ever allowed her to choose her own programmes. The novelty of continually changing channels occupied the rest of the evening.

After three days and nights in the Buenos Aires Guest House, Carly had finished the twenty-five bags. Each morning she would visit the breakfast room and eat a substantial cooked breakfast. Rachel would chat to her, and Carly wallowed in the luxury of being waited on. She learnt that anything she used from her tea tray each day would be replaced. Aware that she might soon be homeless again, she stored whatever sachets she felt it was reasonable to take and began to plan. She spotted the accommodation pages in the remains of her newspaper and was shocked by the high prices. She doubted her benefits would even stretch to a room in a shared house. A funeral announcement caught her eye. 'Celebration of the life of Matthew Johnson, at St Michael's Church, Bexhill, and afterwards in the Church Hall. 26th July 2017 2 pm.' There was much to do. Carly texted Camilla.

Any chance I could meet you today by the market in Hastings at 2pm?
No problem. You okay?
Fine. I have the 25 bags.

Carly felt proud. She tucked the examples of accommodation adverts in her pocket, and packed the cloth bags in her case. The walk to Hastings took two hours, and Camilla was waiting. "You look so well. Where have you been?"

"In a B and B, but I'm only booked for two more nights."

"They'd probably take you back at Orchid House. They knew you were scared, and Donna was chucked out after you left. Frances told me to say, if I saw you, that no one has come looking."

Carly paused. "I don't want to go back. For the first time in my life, I feel like a grown up. I just need to rent a room."

"Can you afford it?"

"Eventually, with my benefits, and the money from selling the bags, but not yet." She showed Camilla the newspaper accommodation adverts.

"They might reduce your benefits if they find you're selling bags."

"Then I won't tell them, at least not until I sell a few more."

Camilla took Carly's case and pulled it over to the stallholder. She unzipped the front and produced a bag. "Here you are, twenty-five bags, as agreed."

The stallholder examined several of the bags in detail. "These are very good. £2 each, yes?" He handed Camilla £50 cash. "If they sell well, I'll take more next time. Tell your friend to come back in two weeks." Camilla walked back to Carly and gave her the money.

"I should charge you commission, but I won't. This is just a start, Carly. You can go into business."

The girls sat on a bench on Hastings seafront and shared a bottle of water which Camilla had brought from Orchid House. Camilla explained to Carly how she would be leaving for university at the end of the summer, and Carly told Camilla about sleeping rough, about the guest house and about the sewing machine. She missed out the bit about the funeral. "I've only got two more days, and after that I'll be homeless again, and I want to change my hair, in case Paul comes looking."

Camilla was thoughtful. "Go back to the guest house. Make as many bags and animals and anything else you can manage in the next two days, as samples. Then if push comes to shove, you'll have to come back to Orchid, just until you find your feet. I miss you." The girls parted company. Carly walked along the promenade in the direction of Bexhill, still clutching the £50. She took several photos on her phone of the displays of summer flowers before diverting to the seafront path. She began to design her next sewing project in her head, before finding her way back to the guest house.

She designed and cut and sewed all evening and rose early the following day to continue, breaking only for breakfast. At midday

Carly dressed in her suit, grabbed her tourist map of Bexhill and started the journey to St Michael's Church. Some time later she walked back from the church hall to the guest house with her bag full of sausage rolls and sandwiches. The following morning, she packed her case ready to check out after breakfast. Rachel was especially attentive. "I'll be sorry to see you go, Carly. I wish all our guests were like you. Your room is always tidy, and you are so quiet."

"I have to go home," Carly lied. There was no home. She paid Rachel in cash at the reception desk. "This is for you to say thank you for lending me the sewing machine." In Carly's hand was a bunch of the most exquisitely hand-sewn fabric tulips. Carly had invisibly strengthened the inside of the stems with strips of plastic cut from a container of noodles. Rachel's eyes filled with tears. "These are beautiful. It's a long time since anyone gave me flowers."

Carly wheeled her case to Bexhill station. The barrier was open, so she walked onto the platform without a ticket. She began to feel very despondent when, half an hour later, she was dragging her suitcase up the hill towards Orchid House. She pressed the bell and was buzzed in. Frances was waiting in the office for her. "Enter." Carly took a seat in the office. "I suppose you expect me to welcome you back," began Frances.

"I know I was wrong to run away, but I was scared. I still am scared."

Frances was disarmed by the apology. "We can protect you, Carly. You have to trust us."

"I don't think I trust anyone. What if Paul comes to Hastings to look for me?"

"In my experience, they rarely do." Carly burst into tears. In an unusual act of compassion, Frances spared Carly her usual lecture and sent her straight to her new room. Nevertheless, Frances felt uneasy, because she realised Carly could be right. This was the first time one of their girls had been pursued by a private detective. She also knew that their volunteer had ignored her training and given too many details over the phone. There was just a chance that Carly could be at risk. Frances turned to her computer and moved Carly's name to the top of the charity's priority housing list. She annotated the entry with the words 'Not Hastings'.

Two weeks later Carly was invited to view a subsidised bedsit in a multiple occupancy Edwardian house in Bexhill. She accepted the move gratefully, and the charity paid for a large taxi to transport her belongings from the hostel to her new home. "After this, you'll be on your own, Carly. We only subsidise you for six months," Frances had emphasised. "You can continue to attend workshops at Orchid House, if you want, but there'll be no more financial support."

"I'll manage. I always manage. And thank you." Frances had always appreciated Carly's good manners. She momentarily showed some emotion and gave Carly a hug.

"You look after yourself."

CHAPTER TWENTY-FOUR

A Home of Her Own

Camilla helped Carly carry her bags downstairs. "Is this all?" asked the driver. "You haven't got much."

"One more favour, though," asked Carly, "could we stop at the sewing shop in Queen's Road?"

"You making curtains for your new home?" teased the taxi driver.

"I left a deposit on a second-hand sewing machine yesterday," Carly explained. "I need to pay the balance and pick it up."

"No problem." The driver stopped outside the sewing shop and switched on his hazard lights, while Carly entered the shop. She emerged a few minutes later carrying the heavy box which contained the machine. Her face broke into a broad smile. "You look happy," remarked the driver.

"This is my future," announced Carly to the slightly bemused taxi driver. He was accustomed to providing transport for the girls from Orchid House, but decided that Carly was not like the others.

They arrived in Bexhill, and he helped her carry her belongings up the stairs to the second-floor room. She found herself alone in her new home. It consisted of a large L shaped room with a double bed, separate settee and kitchenette. The shared bathroom was just across the landing. Carly had spent most of her 'bag' earnings on the sewing machine, but her benefits had been transferred to her new address, and she had been awarded a £50 charity grant for extras. She looked around the room. It had been recently decorated and was immaculately clean. Apparently someone would be sent by the landlord that afternoon to ensure that everything was in good order. Carly inserted the electric key and made a note of the number on the gas meter. She turned the taps on and off and checked that the hot water heater and the fridge were working. She opened the cupboards and drawers and realised they were completely empty. She sat on the bed and began to write a list. She still had the sachets of coffee and milk which she had saved from the guest house, but without a kettle or a mug, they were of no use to her. She double-checked the lock on her door and began to unpack her bags. There was a tap on the door. "Who's there?"

"I'm Holly from across the landing," said a female voice. "We share a bathroom." Carly nervously opened the door. "Can I come in?" Holly was in her mid-thirties. She glanced around the bedsit. "They've done this place up well. It was in a right state."

"It seems lovely," replied Carly, "and very clean. I would offer you a coffee, but I don't have a kettle or a mug. I can't go out and buy anything, because someone's coming from the landlord."

"Make sure you tell him anything you want done," advised Holly. "After the first visit, it's much harder to change things." Holly sat down on the settee. "This is comfortable, must be a new one. The last tenant was on the game, kept smashing things up. I think they evicted her." She stood up and pushed down on the bed. "I see they've left the old mattress. They might replace it, if you ask."

"I don't really need a double bed," explained Carly. "A single would give me more space."

Holly looked surprised. "Most of the girls your age insist on a double. Ask whoever comes. They might change it for you."

Holly stood up. "I don't have a spare kettle, but I'll bring you a mug of coffee. Keep the mug until you can buy your own." Holly walked out, and Carly locked the door behind her. When Holly returned with the coffee, Carly let her in. "You're very security conscious," observed Holly. "If you're nervous, why not ask them to put a chain on the door? There is an entry phone, but the other tenants let anyone in."

"Thank you," said Carly, "I'll ask."

Holly returned to her own room leaving Carly to finish unpacking.

At 3 pm there was a knock on her door. Carly unlocked it and opened the door ajar. She saw a man wearing ID and carrying a large tool box. She let him in. "I didn't hear the entry bell."

"Sorry, the main door had been left open. I just walked in." He looked around the bedsit. "They've done a good job here. The place was in an awful state. Is everything working properly?"

"Seems to be," responded Carly.

"Any requests then? Not that I'm promising."

Carly paused. "Could I have a chain on my door?"

The man looked at her. She seemed nervous. "I think I've got one in my van. I can do it now. Anything else?"

"Well, you'll probably say no but is there any chance you could replace the bed?"

He felt the mattress. "It is a bit lumpy. Not surprising considering its history. You want another double?"

"A single would be better. Give me more space."

"You absolutely sure, love? I'm not trying to interfere, but you might want someone to stay, and they won't change it back again."

Carly's face showed no emotion. "I'm certain."

"I'll see what I can do then." The man went down to his van and returned with a drill and a door chain. When he had finished, he turned to Carly. "I rang your landlord. They'll change the bed at the weekend. Have the office got your number?"

"I think so."

Carly thanked the man again, and he left. She suddenly realised she didn't even know his name. She looked at the time on her phone. She had a small amount of spare cash, and there was just time to reach the shops before closing time. She picked up her keys and left the room, locking the door behind her.

It was only a ten-minute walk into town. Carly bought a few basic provisions and a small bottle of milk before wandering around the shops. She remembered seeing a small electrical outlet when she was staying at the guest house, but feared it might be expensive. She had also noticed a large number of charity shops. She located the electrical shop and looked at the prices of kettles. As she feared, they were expensive. She went into a charity shop and asked about kettles. "We aren't allowed to sell them, but the hospice shop round the corner does. They have a central PAT testing system." Carly had no idea what PAT testing meant, but she headed for the hospice shop and walked inside. It contained a treasure trove of crockery, cutlery, and small household items. There were even a few inexpensive TVs. *Maybe next year*, Carly said to herself. She had noticed an aerial point on the wall in her room but was also aware of the cost of a TV licence. She spotted a box of blankets and sleeping bags and realised she had no bedding. By the time she left the shop, she was carrying two large plastic bags containing a sleeping bag, kettle and various household items. Despite the weight of the bags, she felt a new sense of well-being at the thought of finally creating her own home. Back in her room, she began to empty the bags into her cupboards, taking time to decide how everything should be organised. She had picked up a discarded local newspaper on her way home, and left it open on the 'funeral notice' page to read with a coffee when she needed a break.

CHAPTER TWENTY-FIVE

A New Look

The relationship between Carly and Camilla had always been reciprocal, in so far as Carly needed advice and support, and Camilla needed to feel useful. Both girls were on a slow journey recovering from abuse, but, until Carly moved away from the hostel, they had actually shared very few personal details about each other. There had been an unwritten rule at Orchid House that the girls did not question each other about their backgrounds. Some of the residents were unpredictable and volatile, and too many intrusive questions could easily spark off an incident. That first afternoon when Camilla paid Carly a visit, she sat on Carly's settee drinking coffee, and a growing intimacy began to emerge between them which resulted in greater trust. Camilla started, "You seem much happier here. I mean you've never seemed unhappy, but you always just accepted that people had a right to tell you what to do."

"It's being brought up in care. You're considered to be a responsibility, rather than a person. I just got used to it. And when Brenda stepped down, Paul took over."

"But in lots of ways you're not at all like the other girls I met at the hostel who had been in care. Most of them were really moody."

Carly reflected, "It's because most children in care are moved around a lot. I was sent to Brenda's when I was six and stayed until

I was eighteen. I was lucky. For a looked-after child, I had a pretty stable upbringing. And I didn't have to keep changing schools. Brenda made me knuckle down, so I even got some A-levels, and a vocational qualification in textiles."

"Are you still in touch with your mum?" Camilla dared to ask.

"I lost contact when I moved in with Paul. That's one of the reasons why I kept Carly as my first name, when I came to Sussex. I wanted to hang on to a small part of my history. What about your family?"

Camilla hesitated. "My mum wouldn't believe me when I finally told her about Dad. She accused me of lying. The only way round it would have been to tell the police, and I didn't want my dad to go to prison. That's why I ran away, as soon as I was eighteen."

"Aren't you worried he might do it to someone else?"

Camilla shook her head. "You sound like my counsellor at Orchid. Look, I know this sounds selfish, but I don't want to feel Dad's my problem anymore. I just want to move on. That's why I stayed at Orchid. They weren't like Social Services. They didn't put me under pressure to disclose."

Carly changed the subject. "Do you think Chelsea would come here and do my hair?"

"I'm sure she would. Are you not happy with it? I like your hair."

"I want to look different, I mean really different. So if Paul does come looking, he won't recognise me. I'm forever looking over my shoulder in case he's following me."

Camilla laughed. "We'll have to redesign you then. It sounds like fun!"

A few days later, Chelsea and Camilla arrived with a bag full of old towels and hair dye. Chelsea followed Carly into the bathroom, and Camilla could hear occasional giggles through the wall. When they opened the bathroom door, Camilla looked at the mess in the bath. "I hope this stuff comes off."

"It will," promised Chelsea, "though it might need a bit of a scrub." She wrapped Carly's head in a towel and led her back into her room. Chelsea made Carly sit on the old-fashioned upright chair which she had purchased to use with her sewing machine. "Now I just need to fold this plastic bag around your head, and then you have to sit still for a while." Carly stared at the pile of light brown hair on the floor. "The rest can come off after I've done the colour," Chelsea had explained. "What about the mess in the bathroom? I don't want to upset Holly."

"I'll knock and explain," offered Camilla. "She'll understand."

While Camilla spoke to Holly, Chelsea boiled the kettle. "Are you happy here? D'you get lonely?"

"I really like it. It's the first time ever I've had my own place. I can do whatever I want. I'm saving up for a TV. How long before you move out of Orchid, Chelsea?"

"Three weeks. I started as an apprentice at the Hairline salon last week. Orchid said I could have a month to settle before they rehoused me."

"Are you looking forward to it?" Carly asked.

"I'm a bit nervous, but yes, it'll be good. With Camilla off to uni, and you going, Orchid won't be the same."

Camilla overheard the conversation. "That's their job. Orchid House is just a stepping stone. I know Frances is a tyrant, but she's done well by us."

"P'raps we should buy her a present," suggested Chelsea, "not that we can afford much."

"How about some of these?" Carly produced three hand-sewn cloth irises from the pile of sewing next to her sewing machine.

Camilla and Chelsea admired the flowers. "These are gorgeous. You are so clever. How long would it take you to make a bunch?"

"A couple of days."

"Do you want money for material?"

"I've got loads of material. Holly had a clear-out and gave me some clothes I can cut up. I don't want your money. Call it payment for my hairdo."

Chelsea checked Carly's head. "You're done, by the way. Back to the bathroom now for a wash."

When Carly reappeared, her hair was totally black. Chelsea borrowed Carly's dressmaking scissors and began to cut. She wouldn't let Carly look in the mirror until the cut and blow-dry were complete.

"There, what d'you think?" Carly was stunned. Her long brown hair had been replaced by a head of black elfin spikes which enhanced the shape of her face.

"I really like it, but do I still look like me?"

"You look like Audrey Hepburn," announced Camilla.

"Who?" asked Chelsea and Carly.

"You know, *Breakfast at Tiffany's*."

Carly shrugged her shoulders. "Can I show Holly?"

She knocked on Holly's door. "Wow," said Holly, "that's amazing. You look just like Audrey Hepburn."

PART THREE

CHAPTER TWENTY-SIX

Champagne with Alison

Once the school summer holiday arrived, Martin spent much of his time at Angie's flat. When they were not called upon to look after Joe, they occupied most of their days in Bexhill simply enjoying each other's company. One of their first outings was a visit to Alison's house. Now she was allowed to drink alcohol again, Angie and Martin decided to take her a bottle of champagne.

Alison was looking out for them from her front window. She watched Martin park Angie's car and open the passenger door for her. She whistled quietly as Martin stood up. "You've done all right for yourself there, my friend," she spoke to herself out loud before opening the front door.

Angie hugged her friend. "You look a lot better than when I last saw you."

"I am much better. Sometimes I think the doctors were just having a joke at my expense." Martin kissed Alison on the cheek. She felt herself blush. "So, at last I get to meet the famous Martin. No wonder she's been hiding you away."

"I'm sure she wouldn't mind sharing me," Martin grinned.

"I haven't got that much energy," Alison replied, "but I am allowed to dream." She disappeared into her kitchen and fetched some champagne glasses. "You driving back?" Alison called out to Angie.

"No, we'll leave my car here, and walk home. Martin can drop me off to collect it tomorrow."

"Champagne all round then." Martin stood by the open front door and released the cork. It flew into the road, narrowly missing Angie's car.

"That could have been expensive," he muttered, and then came back into the lounge and filled the three glasses.

"We should have a toast!" announced Alison. "What shall we drink to?" There was an awkward silence, as Angie and Martin imagined a future without Alison.

Angie rescued the situation. "To Alison's bucket list!" They tapped their glasses together.

"And bugger the oncologist," added Alison loudly. "Bugger the oncologist," they all chorused.

"So has your bucket list changed?" enquired Angie.

"Not really. It's just got a bit fuzzier. These latest pills have addled my brain. I'm planning a holiday with Susan. We thought we might rent a cottage in Wales."

"You don't want to go abroad then?" asked Angie.

"Too much worry for Susan, in case I take a turn for the worse."

Angie realised that Alison's condition was never far from her friend's thoughts. "Wales is nice."

"Bloody boring if you ask me," Martin's comment took them both by surprise. "Wales is full of sheep, and it rains a lot. Why don't you go to London and take a trip up the Shard?" Angie realised he was trying to lighten the conversation.

Alison laughed. "You're right. A cottage in Wales does sound dull, but Susan wanted to do it, and it'll only be for a week. Apparently it's important to her that we have quality time together." Angie and Alison laughed, remembering how different the two sisters were. "How are the wedding plans coming along?" asked Alison.

"Very expensive and at times even more boring than the prospect of a week away in Wales. Charlotte talks about nothing else."

"What are you going to wear?"

"God knows… a big hat which hides my face."

"Everyone will want to see your face." Martin topped up their glasses.

Alison turned to Martin. "Have you managed to charm Charlotte yet?"

"Nope, though to be fair, I haven't seen much of her. Joe and I are great mates though."

"Joe adores Martin," added Angie. "He won't stop talking about him."

"He doesn't have any other older men in his life. I think I'm a bit of a novelty," explained Martin.

"Well, Robin wouldn't have been very good with Joe, though no doubt he'd have spent a lot of money on him," said Alison.

"No chance of me doing that on a teacher's pay."

Alison realised she had touched a nerve and changed the subject. "Do you like gardens, Martin? Would you like to see mine?"

"I'd love to."

She stood up, and Martin followed her. Alison took Martin's arm, and together they explored the beautifully-maintained garden. "I've never had children, you see, so this garden is rather like my baby. I worry what will happen to it when I'm gone."

"Your garden will live on in our memories, as you will."

Alison squeezed Martin's arm. "You will look after Angie, won't you? I wouldn't want to see her hurt."

"I love her, Alison. I will always be there for her."

"You should tell her that."

"I'm just waiting for the right moment." Alison and Martin returned to the lounge.

Alison sat down and suddenly looked tired. "Would you mind if I had a rest now?" Angie and Martin said their farewells.

"Well, that wasn't as easy as I expected," sighed Angie, as they strolled back to her flat. "She seemed a bit spaced out to me."

"Probably the medication, and it's not like we're used to talking to people who know that they're dying. I found it really hard."

"What did she say to you in the garden?"

"She opened up a bit. I got a lecture about looking after you," he grinned, "which, of course, I will." He paused again. "Angie, don't be too upset, if Alison doesn't make it to the wedding. She was putting on a good show, but I didn't think she seemed at all well." Angie found herself quietly crying. Martin handed her a tissue. "I'm sorry, I didn't mean to upset you."

"No, you're right. It feels as if she's slipping away from me."

CHAPTER TWENTY-SEVEN

Falling Out

Charlotte was totally preoccupied with the wedding and regularly dropped into the flat to update her mother. However, despite Martin's best efforts, the long silences between Charlotte and himself continued. It was as if Charlotte had built an invisible wall between them. If he sat on the settee, she chose a chair. If he entered the kitchen, she moved to the living room. If Martin began to speak, Charlotte put on her earphones. She walked a careful tightrope between icy responses and downright rudeness. Angie was mortified. "I'm so sorry, Martin. Jess was so lovely to me, and, in a way, she has more excuse to resent me. Her mother is still alive. Robin is dead, and Charlotte needs to move on."

Martin was always surprised at the directness with which Angie spoke about Robin's death. "Look, I loved Robin, and Charlotte adored him, but he was very self-centred. He always had something to prove. He believed he had been disinherited by his grandfather, and the grievance never went away. He poured his unconditional love onto Charlotte, spoiled her, because he needed a family who valued him. It was left to me to set boundaries for Charlotte, to be the strict one. She is the product of his over-indulgence. I can't change that, but I will not let Robin control my future happiness with you through Charlotte. It is not her role to choose my friends," Angie paused, "or my lovers."

Before Charlotte had realised that Angie and Martin's relationship was becoming serious, she had made it clear to Angie that she did not need help from her mother with organising the wedding. Angie's role was to be confined to listening to Charlotte describing every detail and providing transport or child-minding when required. Once Martin appeared on the scene, Angie noticed that Charlotte seemed to need her mother more. Angie's opinions were suddenly important. "What should I do about the flowers, Mum? Will you come with me to choose my dress?" More worryingly, Angie noticed Charlotte repeatedly asking how often Joe would be spending time with Martin. When Angie offered to have him, Charlotte's first question was always, "Will that man be there?"

"Does it matter?" Angie would ask.

"No, of course not, Mum, but Joe does like to spend time alone with his grandma."

Ollie was becoming increasingly irritated by the constant focus on the wedding. Nevertheless, he did agree with Charlotte that the invitations needed to be dispatched as a matter of urgency. Charlotte and Ollie each compiled a list in three parts, family, friends, and work and underlined those names which could be left out of the wedding itself, and just invited to the evening. With both parents passed away, Ollie consulted his uncle about the family guest list on his side, and the matter was quickly sorted. Charlotte drafted a list for her side of the family and then rang her mother to ask for advice. "Our family's so complicated, Charlotte, let me think about it for an hour or so. Why don't you both pop round later for a cuppa. Is Joe with you?"

"Yes, we've planned a walk in Highwoods this morning, so he can run off some energy. We're going to take a picnic, wanna come?" Angie declined. Martin was with her, and she wasn't sure if Charlotte would want him to join the outing. She had more than once considered confronting Charlotte about her negative attitude towards Martin, but Martin had urged Angie to give the relationship more time. As arranged, Ollie and Charlotte knocked on the flat door in the early afternoon. Angie opened the door.

"Where's Joe?"

Joe jumped out from behind Ollie's legs waving a large stick which he had picked up in the woods. "Sorry, he insisted on bringing half the forest back with him," Ollie apologised.

"We love a bit of forest. Come on in. I'll put the kettle on." Joe saw Martin standing in the living room. He dropped the stick and hurtled towards him. "Grandpa Martin, we've been to the woods."

Martin lifted Joe up, so their faces were level. "Well how lovely! Come into the kitchen, and you can tell me all about it. You want squash? I might even be able to find a biscuit, if that's okay with Mummy."

Charlotte did not respond, so Ollie replied, "That's fine, Martin."

Martin lowered Joe to the floor and led him by the hand out of the living room. Ollie was tired after the walk and couldn't resist needling Charlotte. "Martin has made such a hit with Joe, hasn't he, Charlotte?" There was an icy silence. Not for the first time, Angie wondered whether Charlotte's attitude was partly triggered by jealousy of Martin's relationship with Joe

"It's nice for him to have an older male figure in his life," she added provocatively.

Charlotte changed the subject. "This is my invitation list, Mum. Have I missed anyone out?" She passed the handwritten paper to Angie, and Angie ran her eyes over the list. She was pleased that Charlotte had remembered to include Alison. "What does it mean if someone is underlined?"

"They're the people who will only be invited for the evening."

Angie looked directly at her daughter. "I think you've underlined Martin's name by mistake."

"No, Mum, it's not a mistake. I thought, as he's not really family, it would be better if he just came in the evening, out of respect for Dad." Martin was standing in the kitchen doorway, listening.

"And did you not consider my feelings, and Martin's?" Angie's face was growing red.

"I warned you not to do this, Charlotte," interrupted Ollie. "You have to accept that people move on."

"But I don't want him at my wedding, taking Mum's attention and pretending to be family. Joe's even calling him 'Grandpa' now." Charlotte was on a roll. "I can't bear to think of him sleeping with Mum. It's disgusting. Two old people having sex. If that man is at the wedding it will ruin my day," Charlotte continued. Unable to stop herself, she addressed Martin. "You don't mind, do you? After all, you haven't known Mum long. It's my wedding day, and you wouldn't want to ignore my feelings."

Martin picked up his car keys and walked towards Charlotte. "You have made your feelings very clear, Charlotte. Joe's in the kitchen with a drink. Someone needs to keep an eye on him."

Martin walked out of the flat, and slammed the door. No one moved or spoke until Angie finally stepped into the kitchen and sat with Joe. She heard Ollie raise his voice. "You've gone too far, this time, Charlotte. You've always been self-centred, but this wedding has turned you into a megalomaniac." He walked into the kitchen and spoke gruffly to Joe, "Come on, Joe, we're going, and leave that bloody stick behind!" Ollie grabbed Charlotte's hand and pulled her out of the flat with Joe following.

Angie found herself alone. She picked up the stick from the kitchen floor and took it out onto the balcony. She just caught a glimpse of Ollie's car speeding along the seafront and hoped he wouldn't drive too irresponsibly. Feeling completely numb, she returned to the living room and began to clear up the mugs. A few minutes later, there was a tap on the front door. Angie opened the door with caution. It was Martin. He stepped inside. "I was sitting outside in your car. I saw them go."

Angie burst into tears. "I thought you'd run away."

Martin found a tissue and wiped Angie's eyes. "I'm sorry I walked out. I was just so angry, angry for you. You don't deserve this."

"I don't know what to do. Charlotte's always been tricky, but I can usually bring her round. This wedding's turned her into a prima donna."

"If there is a wedding…" Martin looked worried.

"You think they'll call it off?"

"Ollie was not happy." Martin shook his head. "Look, Angie, I never meant to cause you so many family problems. If you want me to leave, just say. It's not fair on you to have to go through all this."

Angie looked startled. "Do you want to leave?"

"No, I don't want to leave." He thought for a long time, while he paced the floor. Angie watched and worried. Eventually he turned and spoke. "I didn't want to say this now. I wanted to wait for a more romantic moment, but say it I must. You are very, very special to me. I have fallen in love with you, completely and utterly. I will do anything for you and put up with whatever crap your family throw at me. But if it's too much for you, I will disappear to Eastbourne until you feel you can cope, forever even."

Angie stood up and put her arms around Martin's waist. "Please don't go. I need you." She took a deep breath. "I love you too, Martin, I really do." He kissed her gently, then passionately, and pressed his body against hers. He slipped his hand under her top and she could feel his breathing quicken. "According to Charlotte, our behaviour is disgusting," laughed Angie.

"It's disgustingly wonderful." Martin took Angie's hand and led her into the bedroom. He laid her onto the bed and slowly removed each individual item of her clothing, taking his time and kissing each part of her body as he progressed. "We could show those youngsters a thing or two." Their eventual climax released much of the earlier tension, and they drifted into sleep.

There was a loud bang on the door, and the bell rang repeatedly. Angie grabbed her dressing gown and walked into the hall. She tied the belt to keep the dressing gown closed before opening the door. Charlotte stood on the doorstep with a suitcase beside her. Joe was holding her hand. "He's chucked us out."

Martin appeared, ruffled, but fully clothed, in the bedroom doorway. "Your mum was about to have a shower. Let's give her a few minutes to dress while I make you a cuppa. You want the toy box down, Joe?" He looked at Angie, who mouthed a 'thank you' and disappeared into the bedroom. Ten minutes later, they were all sitting in the living room drinking tea. Charlotte looked at her feet, and blew her nose repeatedly. Martin put down his teacup, and spoke to her. "Am I allowed to take Joe to the beach? I think you and your mum need to talk."

"You don't have to go, Martin," said Angie.

"I do, just for an hour or so. It will give Joe a break too." Joe had already removed the stick from the balcony, and was tapping it up and down on the carpet.

"Thank you, that would be good," Charlotte said quietly.

"Come on then, mate, let's hit the beach. Grab your clogs from the cupboard, and I'll fetch a towel. That stick can find a new home in the pebbles. You must stay with me though. Your mum doesn't need to worry about your safety." Joe rushed to the hall cupboard and grabbed his beach shoes. He came back into the living room and held out his hand to Martin.

"Ready?"

Martin stood up. "Looks like I'm gonna have to be." He picked up his key and a towel, and the pair left the flat.

Charlotte looked at her mother. "I suppose you want an apology."

"Only if you want to apologise, Charlotte."

"I don't know what I want. You and Ollie can't make me like him. I can't help the way I feel."

"Charlotte, do you actually dislike Martin, or is it just that you don't want me to have a relationship with a man?"

"I don't know. I mean, why do you need to have a man, at your age? Can't you just be a grandma? Aren't Joe and I enough for you?"

"Being friends with Martin doesn't mean I love you and Joe any less." She chose her words carefully. "I'm not quite ready yet to sit at home knitting." Charlotte didn't reply, so Angie continued, "Are you going back to Ollie this evening, or do you want to stay here?"

"I don't think he'll have me back."

"Give it time, Charlotte. You probably both said things you didn't mean."

"We've never really rowed like that before. You and Dad never argued, did you?"

"Oh for goodness sake, Charlotte, we argued all the time. We just hid it from you."

"What did you argue about?"

Angie thought, *about you mostly*. "Come on, let's sort out Joe's room and then make up your bed. Bring the case." Angie pulled out some sheets from the hall cupboard and took them into the spare room. Charlotte followed her.

"I'm sorry to be so much trouble, Mum."

"You don't stop loving your kids, just because they grow up." Angie took a deep breath. "Martin will be staying tonight as well." She just stopped herself asking Charlotte if that would be okay. By the time Martin and Joe had returned, the bedrooms were sorted. Angie lifted up a very sandy Joe and stood him in the bath. "Charlotte, come and shower Joe's feet. Use the towel on the rail. Martin and I are going out for a while. There's plenty in the fridge for Joe's tea. I'll bring in a takeaway for the three of us later." Charlotte looked surprised. "See you later, Charlotte." Angie took Martin's hand and led him out of the flat. They stood in silence in the lift. Neither spoke until they were on the seafront.

"Am I allowed to ask where we're going?"

"The Club for a drink. I need one. And I need to talk to you without Charlotte listening."

Once they were settled on The Club's seafront patio with a bottle of wine on the table, Martin took Angie's hand. "This would have been a better setting for me to declare my undying love."

"I hope you're not regretting it already."

"Of course not," insisted Martin, "but I would like an update on Charlotte and Ollie."

"They've had a row, a big row by the sounds of it. Charlotte and Joe are staying over at mine tonight, maybe longer, if that's okay with you?"

"Do you want me to go back to Eastbourne?"

"Of course not. In any case, you're probably already over the limit. I've told Charlotte you're staying. It's my flat, and she stays on my terms."

"You never said that to me."

Angie grinned, "You're different."

Martin squeezed her hand. "I hope I am."

"We won't get much privacy though, while Charlotte and Joe are with us, and she's off work for the next two weeks for the school holidays. Don't get me wrong, I love them to bits, but I'm not used to having them around all day, every day."

"It might not be for long," reassured Martin. "But if it is, maybe we could slum it in Eastbourne for the occasional night. Do you trust her alone in your flat?"

Angie pulled a face. "Looks like I'm gonna have to!"

Wine bottle emptied, they strolled into the town centre, and bought three large portions of fish and chips. By the time they returned to Angie's flat, Joe was fast asleep in bed. Angie unwrapped the food. "Laps or table?"

"Laps," said Charlotte and Martin in unison, and then both laughed nervously. Angie felt a small glimmer of hope.

CHAPTER TWENTY-EIGHT

Beer with Ollie

A few days later, Angie told Charlotte that she and Martin would be staying in Eastbourne for the night. She gave Charlotte a long list of emergency phone numbers, and Martin carried their cases to her car. "D'you think they'll be okay?" worried Angie.

"She's in her mid-twenties, Angie, and she's a good mum. She also has your strength of personality. You have to trust her."

"Do you think Ollie will have her back?"

"That's something I wanted to run by you later." Angie had grown accustomed to Martin's habit of announcing something important that he needed to say several hours before he actually said it. It took two cups of tea at bedtime, before he finally broached the subject. "I've been thinking about Ollie and Charlotte."

"And?"

"I feel responsible. If it wasn't for me, they might still be together."

"You mustn't feel responsible. You've told me often enough to remember they're grown-ups."

"Yeah, I know, but Ollie hasn't got a dad to talk to about stuff." Martin paused. "I thought I might ask him out for a drink, man to man, without Charlotte knowing."

Angie thought for a moment. "I think that's a brilliant idea."

The following evening, while Angie was back at her flat in Bexhill with Charlotte and Joe, Ollie and Martin were sitting together with a couple of beers in a local pub. They discussed football and work and cars, before Martin finally broached the subject of Charlotte. "Do you miss her?"

"Terribly," admitted Ollie, "but not the rows."

"What about Joe?"

"He was like my own. I think about him all the time."

"Then maybe now would be a good time to start talking to Charlotte again," suggested Martin tentatively, "but set some ground rules this time. Don't put her on a pedestal."

The following evening, Charlotte asked her mother if she would babysit Joe while she went out to meet Ollie. Charlotte texted later to say she would stay the night at Ollie's.

CHAPTER TWENTY-NINE

Charlotte Meets Jess

Once Charlotte had returned to live with Ollie, the wedding plans resumed, though in a slightly less dominant way. Charlotte's relationship with Angie improved. She even began to make an effort to talk to Martin, albeit with a certain reticence. Both mother and daughter seemed to understand that they finally had a chance to set aside the previous conflict and worked hard to move things on. Martin had never dared to suggest to Angie that her controlling manner towards her daughter had not helped the situation, but he noticed there was a growing respect on both sides. The wedding invitations were sent out, and Martin was now included on the main guest list. Ollie and Charlotte arranged to take Angie and Joe to look at the venue, and Jessica prepared to appear surprised when Charlotte realised that Martin was her father. She finally warned Martin by telephone the evening before the visit. Martin wondered why Angie had not made the connection, when she first met Jessica, until he remembered how much alcohol both Angie and Jess had consumed on that night.

Ollie drove to the hotel, and Angie sat in the back of his car with Joe. As they entered the grounds, Angie let out a soft whistle. "This is amazing."

"It is, isn't it," agreed Ollie. "We hoped you'd like it." They walked into the hallway. Joe stared up at the high ceiling and suddenly gripped his mother's hand.

"Are there ghosts here, Mummy?"

Ollie howled. "Great big ones, which float in the air."

"Stop it, Ollie," Angie said firmly, "you'll give Joe nightmares." At that moment Jessica emerged from the office.

"Charlotte, Ollie, and…" she hesitated, "Angie?"

"You two know each other?" asked Charlotte.

"Jess is Martin's daughter," explained Angie, and she gave Jessica a hug. "I didn't realise this was where you worked." Angie watched Charlotte turn crimson and gave her daughter some time to recover. "This is such a lovely hotel, and a great venue for a wedding. Martin was going to come with us today, but it would have been a bit of a squash in the car."

"I was planning on inviting him for a coffee next week. You might want to join us, Angie." Jessica turned to Charlotte. "And this must be Joe."

"Say hello to Jessica, Joe," instructed Charlotte. She watched Jessica pull her hair away from her face and began to see the similarity with Martin.

"Do you want coffee?" asked Jessica. "We can go in the drawing room. Then I'll give Angie and Joe a quick tour, if you like?"

"That would be lovely," agreed Charlotte, beginning to regain her composure.

"Are there ghosts here?" asked Joe.

"No ghosts, Joe, but we do have squash, and biscuits if that's allowed?"

Joe looked pleadingly at his mother.

"That's fine, but not too many biscuits." Tina approached with a tray of coffee, a plastic beaker of squash and a plate of chocolate biscuits. Joe was content munching for a while, until Ollie suggested he quickly showed Joe The Orangery and the main staircase, before fetching a football from Ollie's car.

"We can have a kick-around, while Angie gets a longer tour with Charlotte." The mention of football prompted Joe to leave the biscuits, and he and his prospective stepfather went on ahead, before moving outside. Charlotte tried to remember exactly what she had said to Jessica about Martin during their last visit. Jessica, however, remained entirely professional and began the tour. She showed Angie the suite which she would be sharing with Martin after the wedding, then took the mother and daughter down the main staircase which led to The Orangery. "And this is where the marriage will take place. Both our local registrars are very nice, so it's bound to be a good ceremony. It'll be a bit cold in the garden in late November, but we might manage a few photos outside."

"It's absolutely amazing. Thank you so much for bringing me, Charlotte, and thank you, Jess, for the tour."

"Is there anything else you want to know?" asked Jessica.

"Not for me," answered Angie. "What about you, Charlotte?"

Charlotte still looked slightly uncomfortable. "No, I'm fine. I can always ring if I think of anything."

They shook hands and went outside to find Ollie and Joe.

Everyone was unusually quiet on the journey home. Induced by the rhythm of the engine, Joe fell asleep, giving Angie and Charlotte an excuse to sit in silence with their thoughts. As Ollie dropped Angie off, she kissed her daughter's cheek and promised to meet her at Bexhill station in two days' time. Martin had watched Ollie's car arrive. He was waiting in the flat doorway as Angie came out of the lift. Angie shook her head at him. "You knew, didn't you? You knew it was Jess's hotel."

"Not until Jess told me yesterday," Martin confessed, "and she asked me to keep it quiet. Did it go okay?"

Angie giggled. "Charlotte looked very embarrassed. She went bright red when she realised you were Jess's father. But Jess was totally professional, and it is an amazing place."

"Don't tell me too much. I haven't seen it yet."

"Joe thought it might be full of ghosts." Martin made ghost noises at Angie.

"That's exactly what Ollie did." Angie pretended to sigh.

CHAPTER THIRTY

Wedding Dress and Hat

Charlotte had invited her mother to the bridal shop to view the wedding dress she had selected. She suggested that she might help Angie select her own wedding outfit on the same day. Angie found herself wishing that Alison was well enough to accompany her but had graciously accepted her daughter's invitation. Joe was now back at school, and Ollie offered to collect him, so there was no excuse to delay the shopping trip. Mother and daughter met at Bexhill station mid-morning. Once in Hastings, it was a short walk to the wedding shop. Angie was invited to sit on a white sofa, while Charlotte was whisked away by two young assistants to try on the dress. Angie noticed how the assistants both spoke in the same simpering voices. "Oh, you do look lovely," she heard one assistant say in a high-pitched voice, followed by, "We'll just make a little tuck here, so there's no chance of any wrinkling around the boob area."

The other voice then spoke in similar singing tone, "Almost done, are we ready to show the mummy of the bride?" Angie winced. Charlotte stepped out of the large changing room while the assistants adjusted her train. The dress was a simple design in pure white with occasional lace motifs across the low-cut bodice.

"What d'you think, Mum?"

Angie gasped, "You look beautiful." She felt her eyes begin to water. "What are you going to do with your hair?"

"I thought it should be held up with pearl clips. I've seen some in a small shop in Bexhill. I'll show you another day." It seemed to take forever for Charlotte to be removed from her dress, but she eventually reappeared. She hugged her mother. "Thank you for coming, Mum, lunch next? Then it's your turn. What do want, hat or fascinator?"

"I look awful in fascinators. I thought a very large 'mother of the bride' type hat."

They went to the same Italian restaurant that Angie and Alison frequented and ordered some pasta, accompanied by wine. Angie ate in silence, while Charlotte showed her mother a variety of brides' hairstyles which she had saved to her phone. After lunch, they walked to the one department store in the town centre. "I may not buy anything today," Angie warned Charlotte, "but you can give me your opinion on things." They headed to the ladies' department, where a selection of hats were displayed amongst the more formal dresses. Angie tried one on. "Giant mushroom," she announced as she looked in the mirror. Charlotte passed her another.

"Flying saucer," said Charlotte.

Angie tried on a third. "Saucepan," they laughed together.

"Come on, Mum, try on a fascinator, it might suit you."

Angie chose a blue feathery fascinator. "It won't suit me."

"Try it." Angie fitted the fascinator to her head. Charlotte squealed with laughter. "You're right, it doesn't suit you. Take it off!"

Angie found a chair and sat down. "This isn't going well, is it?"

Charlotte shook her head. "The problem is you're expensive. You always buy designer stuff. We're in the wrong place, Mum. Let's go back to the bridal shop and see what they've got." Angie dreaded the thought of being served by the simpering girls, but she followed her daughter back to the bridal shop. "We haven't got an appointment," explained Charlotte, "but we hoped you might spare us a few minutes?"

"Always on hand to serve our brides." Angie winced again.

"We're actually here for my mum," explained Charlotte. "Do you have any hats in stock?" The shop assistant cast an eye over Angie's head. She called through a lace curtain.

"Charlene, have we got any of those wide-brimmed, mummy of the bride hats out the back?"

"Just checking," replied a sing-song voice. A few minutes later Charlene appeared with a beautiful lace-trimmed hat in oyster with a very wide slanting brim.

"Wow!" exclaimed Charlotte. Angie walked over to one of the full-length mirrors and carefully placed the hat on her head. The assistant adjusted the angle for her. "Mum, that's fabulous," Charlotte said.

"Can I ask what colour your mummy of the bride outfit is?" asked the assistant.

"I haven't bought my mother of the bride outfit yet," replied Angie very deliberately.

The assistant ignored her. "Well we can trim our mummy of the bride hats with feathers and lace in any colour you want. Just bring it back with your outfit, and we will do it for you." Angie was enormously irritated by the assistant, but she adored the hat.

"How much?"

"For the trimming?"

"No, for the hat." Angie tried to sound calm.

Charlene fetched an empty hat box and removed the label. She showed it to Angie. "That's a lot of money for a hat. I'm only going to wear it once."

"Nothing should be too good for the mummy of the bride." The assistant's voice seemed to have taken on a new choral quality.

"I'll take it," said Angie, producing a credit card.

"Does Mummy want the box? It's £30 extra."

Even Charlotte was losing patience. "D'you want the box, Mummy?" she asked in a sarcastic tone.

"Yes, I'll take the box as well. Could you hurry, please. We have a train to catch."

Angie and Charlotte finally escaped. "I'm sorry, Charlotte, but that's finished me off. I'll buy my outfit another day."

"You'll have to go back and get the hat trimmed," Charlotte apologised.

"No I won't. I'm a qualified designer. I can deal with the trimming myself." Charlotte knew better than to argue further with her mother, and they caught the next train back to Bexhill.

CHAPTER THIRTY-ONE

Mother of the Bride Outfit

Angie decided not to leave it too long before buying an outfit for the wedding. She made up her mind to travel to Brighton to try and make the purchase. Despite Charlotte's assertion that everything she wore needed to be designer, Angie was more than happy to browse through the numerous rails of clothes which the chain stores of Brighton would offer. "D'you want to come with me?" she asked Martin. "If I invite Alison, I'll have to keep the trip short, in case she gets tired."

"Whereas you can drag me round the shops for hours," Martin remarked amiably.

Angie hesitated. "Would you be upset, if I went on my own?"

Martin looked relieved. "If you go on Saturday, I could invite Ollie over to watch the motor-racing with me, or maybe even Stewart? It's F1 qualifying. Would you mind?"

"Shopping for my wedding clothes doesn't appeal to you then?" Angie grinned.

"If you want me to come and sit patiently and comment on every item you try on, I will comply."

"I'll go on my own."

Martin insisted he would make his own arrangements for food, so Angie caught an early train to Brighton the following Saturday.

The hat was too large to carry safely, but she had taken some photos to match the colours. She walked down the hill from the Brighton station to Churchill Square and entered the shopping centre. Her plan was to make a brief visit to all of her favourite shops before returning to try on any clothes. Aware that it would be much colder in November, she began to search for tailored dresses, which could be matched with a smart jacket. She had no idea what colour to choose, but decided she should avoid anything which clashed with the bridesmaids' purple dresses. In the third shop she came to, she spotted a deep lilac dress, in a classic plain design. She diverted from her original plan, and asked to try it on. The generous cut disguised her thickening waist, and the neckline was a perfect shape to accessorise with a necklace. She purchased the dress. The search for an oyster coloured jacket then began. There was one that appealed to her in the shop where she bought the dress, but Angie decided to keep searching. After over an hour's browsing, she returned to the original shop and bought the jacket.

It was almost midday, and Angie was beginning to feel weary. She found her way to a coffee shop and sat down. While she was waiting for her latte, she phoned Martin. She could hear the noise of cars in the distance. "It hasn't started yet," explained Martin, "they're just on final practice." He moved into the kitchen, so he could hear properly. "I've got Ollie here, and Stewart is popping up a bit later. Frank was hovering outside, when Ollie arrived, but I ignored him."

"Whatever you do, don't let him in. You'll never get rid of him." It felt strange for Angie to imagine her flat full of people without her being there. "Have you got everything you need?"

"We're fine. How's the shopping?"

"I've bought a dress and a jacket. Just gotta look for shoes now."

"I expect a fashion show when you get back. I will try and say the right thing."

"You always say the right thing. I should be home about 4 pm."

"Good, I'm missing you. If you want a lift from the station, ring me."

They ended the call. Martin sent Angie a text.

I mean it. Call me for a lift from Bexhill xx

Angie felt relieved that she had not been forgotten, despite the competition from male company and fast cars. The search for shoes after lunch was more difficult. Angie was aware that she could no longer stand comfortably in high heels. The colour needed to be an exact match with the jacket and hat, and the heels low enough for her legs to survive a whole day wearing them. She finally entered the most expensive shoe shop in the centre. An assistant brought over a pair of low-heeled oyster-coloured leather court shoes in her size. She looked at the price and grimaced, but when she tried them on they fitted perfectly. She walked around the shop and examined her feet in the mirror.

"They do look lovely," observed the assistant, "and it is for your daughter's wedding."

"I doubt I'll ever wear them again though. Still you're right, they are perfect." Angie paid the bill.

On the journey home she took a photo of the shoes and texted it to Alison with the words *I almost needed a mortgage to pay for them.*

You only live once came the reply, and Angie blinked away a tear. Once past Eastbourne she texted Martin.

Be in Bexhill in about ten minutes.

I'm on my way.

He was waiting in the concourse as she came through the barrier. He took her bags. "Been busy spending money then?"

"Too much."

"You only live once."

"That's what Alison said when I sent her a photo of the shoes."

"You didn't send me a photo of the shoes. I feel left out."

"I thought you'd be too busy entertaining your man friends."

Martin kissed her on the cheek. "It was okay, but I prefer female company, always have."

By the time Angie returned to the flat, Ollie had gone, and Stewart was carrying an empty beer can into the kitchen. There were two ham baguettes on a covered plate in the kitchen. "We saved these for you," said Stewart. Angie took the plate into the living room, and Stewart said goodbye. "Thanks for a great afternoon, Martin."

"He didn't have to go," observed Angie.

"I didn't want to take advantage. It is your flat after all."

"If I want you here, I have to learn to share it."

"Yes, but it can't be easy. Eat up, and then you can show me what you've bought." Angie rummaged through her jewellery and found a lilac necklace. Then for the first time, she matched up her new outfit with the shoes and hat. She was relieved that the combination worked. She came out of her bedroom, and showed Martin. "It's perfect. You look really great."

"I've just got to add a touch of lilac to the hat. I thought maybe a lilac feather or a flower?"

Martin felt a bit out of his depth. "Are there such a thing as lilac birds?"

Angie rolled her eyes. "They dye the feathers, especially for hats."

Martin grinned. "Sorry, that never occurred to me. We'll have to go in your car though. I don't think that hat would fit in my Fiat." He decided not to say anything else.

CHAPTER THIRTY-TWO

Wedding Flowers

K nowing that Charlotte was still struggling with the idea of a winter bouquet, Angie took a trip to Hastings to find the market stall where she had purchased the hand-made flowers. Sure enough, at the far end of a pedestrianised side street she spotted the green gazebo under which there was a display of cloth animals, bags, and exquisite individually-designed blooms. The stallholder looked vaguely familiar, and Angie supposed it was because of her likeness to the film star Audrey Hepburn.

She examined each of the blooms in detail. "Do you think you could make a wedding bouquet out of some of these?" enquired Angie.

Carly thought for a moment. "Probably, yes, but I'd need to know what flowers... and it would take a bit of time."

"I'd need them by mid-November, and two posies for the bridesmaids. I was wondering if you could make a couple of sample blooms and some greenery for me to show my daughter first to see if she likes them? I'd pay you, of course."

"What flowers and colours?"

"I'll leave the type of flowers to you, but I think the bridesmaids will be in purple satin."

"So maybe some irises and something white?"

"That sounds lovely. When shall I come back? I live in Bexhill."

"So do I," admitted Carly without really thinking.

"We could meet there then. Maybe at a café somewhere?" Angie really wanted to invite the stallholder to her flat, but she seemed a bit nervous. Angie handed Carly her card. "Give me a ring when the samples are ready. How long will that be, d'you think?"

"Two weeks?"

"I'll look forward to hearing from you."

Carly had learned over many years to suppress her emotions, but that afternoon she felt a rare flutter of excitement as she packed up her stall. She moved out of the way to allow Bill from the neighbouring stall to reverse his van through the pedestrian space and park beside her. She loaded her plastic boxes of goods onto his van, as she did every working afternoon. It was a longstanding arrangement which Carly had negotiated when she first took over the pitch. In return she would watch his stall on those mornings when he was travelling to and from suppliers or taken up with other commitments. He didn't say a lot, but one of the other stallholders had told Carly he regularly visited his mother in a care home. Bill helped Carly to unscrew the plastic weights and collapse the gazebo. "You won the lottery? I don't often see you look happy."

Carly grinned. "I've got a commission, for a wedding bouquet."

Bill looked puzzled. "Real flowers?"

"No, daftie, hand-sewn ones."

"That's nice." Bill obviously didn't understand.

"But I'll need to do some research. I've never been to a wedding."

"What never! None of your family ever married?"

"I don't have much family." Carly tended not to give away too many personal details, and Bill realised he had asked one question too many.

"Go and have a word with Liz. She does bouquets. She's probably got some photographs." Carly lifted her gazebo onto

Bill's van, then walked up the roadway to Liz's floristry stall. Liz was beginning to fill metal buckets with bunches of flowers. Carly loved the colours and fragrances which surrounded her stall.

"Bill said you might have some photos of wedding bouquets?"

"You getting married?"

"Not ever," Carly insisted. "This posh woman wants me to make a material bouquet of flowers for her daughter, and some posies. Apparently it's a winter wedding, and she wants something different."

Liz thought for a few seconds. "D'you know, I think that's an amazing idea. If you get this one right, it could take off, and your flowers are much nicer than that artificial rubbish which most of the cheap shops are stocking." Liz pulled out a folder from the back of her stall. She showed Carly the plastic-covered photographs of bouquets of flowers constructed in varying shapes and colours. Carly was surprised at how high the prices were. "I can't lend you this folder, but it will give you an idea. You can probably print off loads of pictures from the internet." Carly did not admit to Liz that she could not afford the internet, let alone a printer. She had now been in a bedsit for over a year, but any spare money had been spent on her stall. Camilla had helped Carly access a business start-up grant, but after the first year she was expected to live on the small income from her stall, and trade was likely to drop as winter approached.

That evening Carly phoned Camilla and told her about the bouquet. Camilla was now in her second year of a business studies degree. "This is an amazing opportunity. I've always said you could set up an online shop." Carly had learned to curb Camilla's enthusiasm.

"It's just one wedding, Camilla, not a business empire. And I can't afford the internet."

"But you never know where this will lead. I'll print off a few photos at uni and post them to you. I might be able to find a company which will send you some brochures. You could even prowl round a few churches that have weddings on, see what the latest trends are. D'you think you could do that and stay inconspicuous?"

"I'm sure I could." Two days later, a selection of printed photos of wedding bouquets arrived in the post from Camilla. There were also three separate glossy brochures from online florists featuring expensive bouquets, posies and buttonholes in a wide variety of designs. "Matching buttonholes," Carly said to herself, "now that's an idea."

By the time Carly phoned Angie two weeks later, her eyes were aching through long nights spent experimenting with colours and shapes. But on a small table in her room was a beautiful and delicate selection of hand-sewn blooms wrapped in white and purple tissue paper. Angie arranged to meet Carly at the De La Warr Pavilion café in Bexhill. It was a Monday morning, so Carly's stall was closed. Carly had carefully packed her flowers into a wheeled plastic box and transported them in the lift to the first floor of the Pavilion. Angie was waiting for her in an area of soft seating towards the back of the café. The women shook hands, and Angie fetched two coffees, after which Carly began to unwrap the flowers. She had included photographs of a variety of shapes of bouquets.

"I thought that a combination of white peonies and deep purple irises would fit perfectly with your colour theme, and the inclusion of silver stems of honesty would add another dimension to the shapes. If you do decide you want buttonholes, then it might be a good idea to combine lily of the valley with a single iris."

Angie was enchanted. "I think these are exquisite, and so different from anything I've seen before. Have you seen anything like this at a wedding?"

Carly was disarmed by the compliment. "Actually, I've never been to a wedding, only funerals."

Angie paid for the samples and took Carly's phone number. "I'll need to talk to my daughter, but I'm sure we can do business.

I'll ring you in a couple of days." With the delicate blooms carefully folded into her large leather shopping bag, Angie took the ten-minute walk from the De La Warr Pavilion to her flat. There was a sharp breeze, and Angie stopped by a bench to wrap her scarf around her ears. Carly's face kept intruding into her thoughts. Why was this girl so familiar? Angie was sure she had seen her before.

CHAPTER THIRTY-THREE

The Sandwich Lady

The new term was well underway. Although Martin had indicated to Angie that he would have to return to Eastbourne when he was working, he chose to spend more and more time staying in Bexhill. He began to commute to Eastbourne for work, only returning to his house to collect a few belongings or pick up his post. He had wondered if he might miss his Eastbourne home, but he soon adjusted to the maintenance-free existence which Angie had chosen for herself. However, he found the travelling tiring, and the difference in their income continued to concern him. He knew he would need to work part-time until he could finally access his state pension in three years' time.

When Martin was working, Angie spent her spare time trimming her hat, as well as working on a design commission from one of her clients. On the rare occasions when Martin did stay in Eastbourne, he would wander from room to room not knowing what to do with himself. He also had to admit that he missed the luxury of Angie's flat. The bachelor existence which had once felt cosy now seemed uncomfortable and chaotic. He even found himself watching the TV programmes which Angie enjoyed. Angie was delighted to have Martin back in her home almost full-time, but she noticed that the travel was tiring him. She began to wonder whether she should suggest that Martin sold his Eastbourne home and moved in with her permanently, but she was by no means certain if he felt ready for such a commitment. On the day when Angie had met Carly at the De La Warr, Martin had taken a day's supply with a year nine class at Eastbourne High. He rarely worked on a Monday and had not taught in the secondary sector for some time, but the school was short-staffed and had begged him to help out. He had found maintaining discipline with a group of teenagers much more challenging than he expected. By the time he had eaten the evening meal which Angie had prepared, he was exhausted and fell asleep in the chair. After an hour Angie gently shook his shoulder and suggested he should go to bed. She wanted to tell him about the flowers, but realised Martin was too tired to take anything in. Angie followed shortly after, and it was not long before she too fell asleep.

She woke at 3 am feeling restless. Carly's face had found its way into her dreams, and she was trying to make sense of it. The words 'I've never been to a wedding, only funerals' kept repeating themselves in her head. Her sleep was intermittent, until she eventually gave in to wakefulness and at 5 am disappeared into the kitchen to make tea. The memory of Carly's face at Jack's funeral finally emerged while she was pouring boiling water into a mug. It gave her such a jolt that she dropped the mug of hot tea onto the tiled floor with a loud crash. Martin woke with a start and rushed into the kitchen. He stared at the broken crockery on the kitchen floor. "Are you all right?"

"Sorry, I didn't mean to wake you. I've just had a bit of a shock."

"It must be serious if it makes you throw cups around the kitchen. Sit down, and I'll clear up the mess. Tell me what's happened." And Angie explained to Martin about meeting the girl who makes flowers, and how she had just realised this was the same person who had taken the sandwiches at Jack's funeral. "Are you absolutely sure, Angie, could she not just be very similar?"

"I'm positive. Her face has a look of Audrey Hepburn, you know, in all those lovely films?" Martin stirred his tea. "Does it matter? Will it stop you ordering the bouquet?"

"I don't think so, though I wonder now if I can trust her. Should I mention it?"

"That's your decision."

"What would you do?"

"Me? Well, I have problems shutting up, so I'd probably say something. There might be a perfectly reasonable explanation. Perhaps she knew Jack and just wanted something to eat on her way home."

"Of course, you could be right. It's just she was so... furtive." They took their tea into the living room, and Martin stepped out onto the balcony. Ribbons of light were beginning to emerge above the horizon, in anticipation of the sunrise. Angie fetched her dressing gown and joined Martin. He put his arm round her. "I do understand why you love this place so much. It sort of grabs you, doesn't it? Like someone is casting a spell." They watched the sunrise, before returning to the bedroom to get dressed. Martin was not working that day, so he suggested that they go out for breakfast. The morning was chilly, but they grabbed their coats and headed for the nearby little café which overlooked the beach. The smell of grilled bacon increased their hunger, and they each ordered a full breakfast and a hot chocolate. "This won't help my diet," said Angie.

"I've told you, you don't need to go on a diet. I like something to get hold of. I know you said that the sandwich lady was pretty, but, if I remember her rightly, she was extremely thin, scraggy even. It's not attractive."

"So you do remember her?"

"Oh yes, I remember her. I can't help looking at women, even at funerals. I just don't remember her taking the sandwiches. I think I was too busy falling in love with you by then." Angie couldn't help but be captivated by the warmth of Martin's affection coupled with his wit. It was a compelling combination.

The following day Martin was working again, so Angie phoned Charlotte to arrange to show her the flowers. Charlotte promised to drop into the flat for lunch. Angie had been very animated when describing the flowers, and Charlotte was worried she might not like them as much as her mother did. She decided it would be easier to let her mum down over lunch. Angie laid the kitchen table out with bread, salad and cold meat. It looked inviting, and Charlotte tucked in as soon as she arrived. Angie ate quickly, then left the table, returning with the bag of flowers. She slowly unwrapped each bloom and showed them to Charlotte. "These are absolutely gorgeous," admitted Charlotte. "I thought they might be a bit tacky, but they are so detailed and delicate. I bet they're expensive."

"Not really," said Angie, not considering the work, "and you can keep them afterwards for your home. If you like them, I'll pay for them, but you'll need to approve the shape of the bouquet. Do you want buttonholes as well?"

"I hadn't even thought about buttonholes, but yes please. The men are wearing purple waistcoats and cravats to match the bridesmaids. I wanted pink, but Ollie said no."

Angie smiled. "Quite right too. I'm not having my grandson wearing pink. I assume you want Joe to match."

"Of course." They browsed through the photographs which Carly had given to Angie, and Charlotte selected her preferred designs. Angie managed to let her daughter make the choices without expressing an opinion. When Charlotte had gone, Angie telephoned Carly. They arranged to meet at the De La Warr later the following day, after Carly had closed her stall for the day. Angie felt anxious as Carly approached. Their conversation began in a business-like manner while Angie described the designs which Charlotte had selected. Prices were provisionally agreed, and Angie asked Carly about payment. "Will you want a deposit?"

"It would be helpful."

Angie took a deep breath. "Before I pay you any more money, there's something I need to ask you."

"Anything."

"I want to know if it was you I spotted at the Beach View Hotel in Bexhill for my Uncle Jack's funeral." Carly grew pale. There was a long silence. Carly was accustomed to lying to keep herself out of trouble, but she sensed that Angie would not be easily fooled.

"Yes, that was me. I'm sorry, I was hungry."

"So you didn't actually know Jack?"

"No."

Carly began to panic that she had lost Angie's business.

"Do you do this often, or was it a one-off?"

"About once a month, but I do have rules. If people are really upset, I don't stay." Angie remembered how no one at Jack's funeral had said a good word about him.

"Don't you make enough money for food from your stall?"

"It barely pays my bills."

Angie looked hard at the pale young woman in front of her. She decided to take a chance. "Are you hungry now?"

"I'm not used to eating much, but I'm always hungry when I think about it."

Angie texted Martin. *What time will you be back from school? I need your help with something.* Angie rarely asked Martin for help, so the request alarmed him. *I'm on my way.*

She looked at Carly. "You were very prompt with the samples, and I want to trust you. But this is my daughter's wedding, and I can't let her down. I need you to tell me a bit more about yourself before I give you any more money. Come back to my flat, and I will make you some dinner. My partner will be there as well." Angie and Carly walked slowly back to the flat, so Angie could ensure that Martin would be there to support her. When they arrived at the flat, Martin's Fiat was parked in its usual space. They took the lift to the fourth floor, and Angie let them both in. "Martin," she called out, "we have a visitor!" Martin appeared from the kitchen. "This is Carly. She's staying for dinner."

Martin looked confused. "Hi Carly, I'll set another place at the table. D'you want a glass of wine?"

Carly hesitated.

"It's okay, Carly, have some wine. What do you like? Red or white?" Angie tried to reassure her.

"White, please." Martin left the kitchen to fetch some wine.

"I'll just go into the living room and check he's found the right bottle," explained Angie.

"What on earth is going on?" Martin whispered to Angie.

"It's her!" Angie whispered back. "She is the sandwich lady. You're good at interrogating people. See what you can find out."

"Thanks a lot, Angie."

He pulled out a bottle of white wine, which he carried to the kitchen. "There's a beef casserole and roast potatoes in the oven. I've just got to reheat it. Is that okay?"

"Sounds lovely." Martin filled her glass and sat down at the table with Angie and Carly.

Angie decided to break the silence. "This is my friend Martin, Carly, but he's also a distant cousin, which is why he was at Jack's funeral." She turned to Martin. "Carly didn't know Jack, but she has explained to me that she occasionally goes to funerals when she is hungry. That's why I offered her dinner."

"Blimey," said Martin light-heartedly, "don't you get fed up with egg sandwiches?"

Carly giggled. "I prefer sausage rolls."

"And you've never been caught out?" Martin's non-judgemental manner and genuine interest broke down Carly's usual reticence.

"Most people don't ask who you are at funerals. If you look confident, and they don't know you, they just assume you are a friend or belong to the other side of the family."

"So, don't you have any family of your own?"

"My mother was a drug addict. I was taken into care when I was six."

"And no doubt passed from one placement to another." Martin knew about looked-after children.

"Actually no, I stayed with the same foster mother until I was eighteen."

"And don't you see her anymore?"

"We lost touch." Dinner was ready, and Martin decided to leave the questions for a while. Carly ate politely, but both Martin and Angie could see she was hungry. Her plate was soon empty. "That was really lovely."

Martin refilled her glass. "You can take the rest of the casserole home with you, if you want. Do you have an oven at home?"

"Oh yes, I'm not homeless. I have a bedsit."

Martin decided to probe a little more. "So how did you end up in Bexhill?"

"I was in a hostel, called Orchid House, in Hastings. They rehoused me." Martin instinctively knew when to stop, and he noticed that Carly was looking tired.

"I've only had one small glass of wine. I'll run you home."

Carly looked at Angie. "Thank you for the food. I don't suppose you want me to make the flowers now?"

Angie hesitated. "I do want you to make the flowers, but I need to discuss a few details first with Martin." She held out two twenty-pound notes. "Take this to buy some materials to make a start. I'll ring you in a couple of days to agree dates and deadlines. We'll get you home now. I'll come in the car with Martin." Angie handed Carly a bag containing a foil carton with the remainder of the casserole. They took Martin's car and dropped Carly off outside her house. Martin made a note of the address. Once they were alone in the car, Angie asked, "What d'you think?"

"I wouldn't like to say. She's obviously managing to run a market stall in Hastings, but she was definitely hungry. You might never see that £40 again," warned Martin.

"I thought I'd give her a few days, then ring and check on her progress. If she's really used my money for materials, then I'm going to trust her. I think I'll set a completion deadline for a couple of weeks before the wedding though, just in case she lets me down, and I have to buy real flowers."

Back at the flat, Martin did a search for Orchid House. He called Angie to look at the screen of his laptop. "Look at this!"

She read the screen. *Orchid House, Hastings, is a hostel run by the New Start charity. It offers short-term accommodation to young women who have been abused by a partner or family member. We aim to find them employment or training and rehouse them within six months.*

"Poor kid," said Angie. "She only looks about Charlotte's age, and she's obviously been through a lot. She's also extremely talented with a needle. It would be a shame if she didn't put it to good use."

"Have you seen this photo?" asked Martin. There was a picture of the Orchid House office on their website. Sitting on the desk was a vase full of Carly's hand-sewn flowers.

Martin sat next to Angie and held her hand. "Just be careful. I've dealt with a lot of troubled kids. They often find it hard to build long-term relationships, because so many people have let them down. She might be on drugs. Don't give or expect too much."

"I promise. I'll be careful."

Two days later, Carly rang Angie. "I thought you might think I'd gone off with your money, so, as a start, I've made the eight buttonholes you wanted. I could bring them round to show you. Bill has offered to watch my stall."

"That would be lovely, Carly. Shall we say about midday?"

"Midday is fine." Angie made sure she had plenty of food in the fridge. Carly arrived on time and rang the outdoor bell. Angie buzzed her in. She was soon tapping on the door. Carly opened up her bag in Angie's living room. "I've been dying to show you." She spread out the buttonholes on the table. Each hand-sewn purple iris was bound together by white cotton with a small stem of lily of the valley and attached to a metal lapel clip.

Angie felt quite emotional. "These are just lovely. How long did they take?"

"Quite a long time, but I got quicker, and I still have some material left for the rest of the irises. I will need to buy more stuff though for the peonies and the honesty."

"These are really high-end goods, Carly, and you need to factor in your time." She sat down with Carly and helped her to price the work properly. "As I'm your first wedding customer, I expect a discount, and I can support you with any future marketing, but you mustn't undervalue yourself. Also, you're working alone, so you must allow sufficient time." Payment dates and schedules were agreed, and Angie offered Carly some lunch.

"I don't want to be any trouble," responded Carly.

"You're no trouble. Martin's working, so I'm on my own." She led Carly into the kitchen where the table was laid out with salad and meat pie. "No egg sandwiches or sausage rolls, I'm afraid." Carly laughed. It had been a relief to tell someone about the funerals. "Do you think you will carry on going to funerals?" Angie asked.

Carly thought for a while. "I don't know. It is a bit of a compulsion, and it's better than shoplifting, which is what some of the Orchid girls did. I mean, the food left over from funerals just goes in a bin, so I'm not taking it from anyone. Though if I begin to earn enough to buy loads of food, I might not want to do it anymore." Angie was amused at the way Carly chose to rationalise her behaviour.

CHAPTER THIRTY-FOUR

The EGM

One of the few disadvantages of living in Angie's flat was that the postman didn't deliver letters to each individual apartment. Letters were left inside the secure mailboxes in the ground floor lobby. If Angie was busy, she often waited until she and Martin went out before collecting the mail. A few weeks before half-term, Martin returned to the flat after a day's teaching and noticed that Angie had still not collected her mail. He used his key to open the box. There was a brown envelope, entitled 'Pacific Flats Newsletter'. He slipped it into his briefcase and carried it up to Angie. "These newsletters are always boring," she remarked, as she opened the envelope. She quickly glanced through the letter. "I see Frank has wheedled his way onto the committee as secretary."

"I don't s'pose anyone else wanted to do it," responded Martin. "Can I see?" She handed over the newsletter. "Oh, it says here, that, as secretary, he is calling an EGM."

Angie looked worried. "That normally means that there's a major maintenance issue."

"No," Martin read out loud, "just one agenda item. 'Breach of lease rules about taking lodgers'."

"He referred to you as my lodger once."

"Did you contradict him?"

"I didn't. It's none of his business."

Martin sighed. "Perhaps he thinks it is. This could be about us you know. Why on earth is he so against me?"

"Jealous," Angie suggested," of anyone who has the good fortune to start a new relationship. Should we do anything?"

"I doubt that's necessary, but I might have a quick word with Stewart. He's on the committee, isn't he? He'll know what's going on."

Martin went down the stairs and knocked on Stewart's door.

"Martin, how nice, come in." Stewart led Martin into his kitchen. It was the first time that Martin had been inside Stewart's flat, and he couldn't help but notice the different layout. "I expect you'll notice how different this place is to Angie's. I've only got one bedroom. She has three."

Martin grinned. "Plenty of room for lodgers…"

"You've heard then?" asked Stewart.

"I read the newsletter."

Stewart took a deep breath. "As a committee, we have to follow the rules. I was surprised though, Martin. I always thought you and Angie were an item, and it's not as if she needs the money."

Martin protested, "We are an item."

"Frank said that Angie had told him definitely you were a lodger. I did think that was a bit strange, having seen you both together."

"He's a bloody liar," retorted Martin. "What does he want me to do, show him my bank account as proof? Or maybe video me and Angie in bed? In any case I still own my house and work in Eastbourne. Why on earth would I want to lodge in Bexhill?"

"Leave it with me," reassured Stewart.

The day of the EGM arrived. These meetings were normally poorly attended, but, by the time Angie and Martin arrived, the community room was almost full. Word had got around that

Frank might get his come-uppance. The chair called the crowd to order. "This is an extraordinary meeting convened in response to a complaint by one of the leaseholders. Our rules state that if a resident's complaint is ratified by at least one member of the committee, then the secretary can call an EGM to discuss it, if appropriate. The committee rule was introduced to stop any one resident being able to call an EGM without good reason. However, in this case the complainant is also a committee member and the secretary, so we felt obliged to allow him to hold a meeting. No other committee members have ratified the complaint. Please bear this in mind if we go to a vote." Martin squeezed Angie's hand.

"The complaint reads as follows: 'That the leaseholder's rule which does not allow subletting or paid lodgers has been breached. It is therefore proposed that the leaseholder concerned should be asked to evict his or her lodger.' The complainant is our newly appointed secretary Mr Frank Watts. Before we proceed are there any questions from the floor or the committee?"

Stewart raised his hand. "Two questions if I may? Firstly, would Mr Frank Watts please be courteous enough to name the alleged guilty leaseholder? Secondly, does he have actual evidence of the breach?"

Frank rose to his feet. "The leaseholder is Mrs Angela Stewart, and she has admitted to me that she has taken a lodger." The room fell silent while people looked at Angie.

"Would you like to respond, Angie?" asked the chair.

"Not really," said Angie. "But in the interests of resolving this matter swiftly, I will speak. Frank, are you prepared to name my alleged lodger?"

Frank pointed to Martin. "That man."

"And at what point did I inform you that this man was my lodger?"

Frank tried to speak with drama in his voice. "I called him a lodger, and you did not deny it."

Angie stood again. "I did not reply, because it was none of your bloody business! Martin Black is not my lodger. He is my lover." There was a spontaneous clap from everyone in the room, except, of course, Frank. The chair called the room to silence.

"Well, unless anyone wants a vote, I think that puts the issue to bed." The room filled up with laughter. "Sorry, bad choice of words."

"I thought it was a great choice of words," someone shouted.

The chair could just be heard to say, "I declare this meeting closed" above the noise of the residents leaving the meeting. Stewart approached Angie and kissed her on the cheek.

"Better than a night's TV."

CHAPTER THIRTY-FIVE

Hens and Stags

Angie and Martin agreed to have Joe to stay for two days during the October half-term. Charlotte was saving up her holiday for the honeymoon, and Angie had discovered that minding Joe when Martin was around was a lot less tiring than when she was on her own. At the end of the second day, Ollie came to collect Joe. He sat down and chatted to Martin. "We should go for a drink again soon," remarked Ollie. "I enjoyed our night at the pub."

"You mean you're allowed out after dark? I'd have to ask your prospective mother-in-law's permission."

Angie came through from the kitchen. "I heard that. You know I can't wait to get rid of you for an evening."

"I'm sure that's how Charlotte feels about me," Ollie continued. "According to Charlotte, it's obligatory for the groom to have a stag night. To be honest I'd rather stay at home with a mug of cocoa."

"They do make such a big deal of these things now, don't they, Ollie," agreed Angie. "Aren't you going to take your mates on a boozy weekend somewhere abroad?"

"Over my dead body," answered Ollie. "As I absolutely have to something, it'll be a meal out and a few drinks. Actually, I discovered this great little café and pizza house in Bexhill which does Greek food as well. They're not licensed, but you can bring your own alcohol. I thought you might like to join us, Martin."

Joe had been playing with his Lego on the floor. He looked up. "Can I come, Ollie? I like pizza."

"Sorry, mate, grown-ups only, more's the pity. I'll have to hope Grandpa Martin is willing to keep an eye on me."

"Sounds great, Ollie, though I can't hold my drink like I used to."

"You'll be in good company then."

When Ollie had left with Joe, Martin asked Angie, "Are you okay with this, I mean me going to Ollie's stag night?"

"Of course I am. It's great that Ollie has invited you. Just don't get arrested for being drunk and disorderly."

"Fat chance of that in Bexhill! So what about you, Angie? Are you to be summoned to a hen party?"

"Charlotte phoned me today. It's next Friday. They're going for a meal then on to a disco and spa weekend. It has been decided that anyone old, like me, need only stay for the meal. And it's in Hastings, so I'll need a taxi."

"I'll pick you up, as long as it doesn't clash with Ollie's stag 'do'."

"I doubt it will. Ollie will be needed to babysit Joe."

The night of the stag 'do' arrived. Martin bought six cans of beer and a bottle of wine which he put in a plastic carrier to take with him. Avra Café and Pizza House was situated in Town Hall Square in Bexhill. The café wasn't large, but a long table was already set out to accommodate the expected ten men who had indicated they would be attending the evening. Ollie's business partner and best man, Mike, was there first, decorating the table with photos of Ollie as a child. The proprietor was putting glasses on the table, while her Greek husband could be heard cooking in the small kitchen area. Ollie had organised the food and taken payment in advance, so all Martin had to do was sit and wait and drink. He put his wine on the table and gave the beers to the best man. The proprietor came, opened his bottle and filled his glass. "This, I assume, is the stepfather of the bride," said the best man with slightly slurred speech.

"I think the best man started early," said Annette, "but no doubt he'll feel better when the food is produced." The stag party guests slowly arrived until the table was full. Annette and her husband began to serve large platters of Greek food for everyone to share. They tucked into the selection of dishes, and used the warm home-made pitta bread to wipe their plates before helping themselves to more. Ollie moved around the table making sure everyone's glass was refilled. He finally sat down next to Martin and refilled his glass.

"I'm so pleased you decided to come." He called Annette over. "This," he declared over-deliberately, "this is the man who saved my marriage."

The best man stood up and hiccupped, "A toast to Martin, the man who saved Ollie's marriage."

Everyone stood, albeit somewhat shakily. "To Martin, who saved Ollie's marriage."

By the time they had finished eating, Martin realised his head was swimming. He couldn't hold his drink like he used to. He tried to stand up and fell back down on his chair. Ollie took Martin's arm. "Come on, old man, we'll walk you home."

"Less of the old," slurred Martin. Someone helped Martin put on his coat, and the best man and Ollie took an arm each. They stumbled into the cold evening followed by three of Ollie's friends from work.

"Safety in numbers, lads," shouted one of them, "let's get the old man home!" The party of five swerved through the normally quiet streets of Bexhill, occasionally shouting out, "To Martin, the man who saved Ollie's marriage." Martin somehow managed to stay upright until he reached the entrance to the flats, where he suddenly sat down on one of the flower beds. The cold air had helped to sober Ollie sufficiently for him to ring the bell.

He spoke slowly into the intercom. "I think Martin might need a helping hand." A few minutes later, Angie appeared and looked at Martin sitting between two large hydrangea bushes.

"Sorry, love," slurred Martin, as he managed to stagger to his feet. Frank appeared in the lobby and stepped outside to investigate the noise.

Mike approached Frank. "This," he announced, "is Martin who saved Ollie's marriage."

Frank looked horrified. "And this drunken display is why I wanted him out of the flats. He has completely lowered the tone of the neighbourhood." Frank stood and faced Martin. "You, sir, are a disgrace!" Martin pulled himself to his full height and looked down on Frank.

"And you, sir, are an interfering twat!" Several residents had come out of their flats to watch the encounter. They cheered loudly as Angie helped Martin into the lift.

Martin woke at 10 am the following morning. He slowly sat up holding his head with both hands, as he began to remember the antics of the previous evening. Angie watched him from the bedroom doorway. "I'll fetch some strong coffee."

Martin rose slowly and walked into the kitchen. "I am so sorry, Angie, I didn't realise how much I'd had to drink. I'm surprised you let me sleep in your bed. You should have banished me to the spare room."

"I thought I'd better keep an eye on you."

He drew close to her. "Are you very cross with me?"

"Not in the slightest, it was a stag night." She pulled a face. "But keep your distance. You smell of stale alcohol." Angie continued. "I wouldn't want you to do it too often, but you were funny, and it was great to see Frank's expression."

"Oh God, Frank, I'd forgotten about Frank. Should I apologise to him?"

"Don't you dare. Anyway, I think he's written you a letter. This envelope was in our mailbox this morning." Angie handed Martin an envelope with Martin's name handwritten on the front.

He sat down and felt it. "There's a small lump. It might contain a bomb."

"Best open it and see." Martin opened the envelope. It contained a letter and two paracetamol wrapped in foil.

Dear Martin,

I hope you are not suffering too much this morning. We really should have another beer together soon. Thanks for the continuing entertainment.

Stewart

Martin took the paracetamol with his coffee and passed the letter to Angie. She laughed. "Stewart is so lovely, and at least the stag night is over. I hope Ollie got home okay."

"He'll be fine. These youngsters are resilient. The problem is that we come from an age where, although we undoubtedly drank too much, we tended to pace ourselves. Kids of Ollie's age don't drink every day, but when they do, they tend to binge. I don't know which is worse, but I couldn't keep up. And speaking of binge, isn't it Charlotte's hen night next Friday?"

Angie pulled a face. "I'm dreading it. It might just be me and a lot of drunk young women."

"Then they won't notice if you leave early. I promised I'd pick you up after anyway." Martin suddenly looked pale. "D'you mind if I go back to bed? I feel awful." Angie followed Martin into her bedroom and tucked him in. "I don't deserve you," he muttered as he closed his eyes.

Selecting her bridesmaids had not been a difficult decision for Charlotte. There were no eligible family members, so her two school friends, Laura and Katy, had been the obvious choice. When Charlotte had fallen pregnant at the age of eighteen, she had been temporarily working with Laura and Katy at a local call centre prior to taking up a place to study accountancy at university. Being unwilling to terminate the pregnancy, Charlotte had given up her university place and stayed on at the call centre until shortly before Joe was born. She had then worked part-time and lived with Angie at the family home until Joe was two, after which she and Joe had moved into a flat with Laura and Katy. It was shortly after this that Angie, suddenly feeling alone, had sold the family home and purchased her three-bedroomed flat at the Pacific block overlooking the seafront. Charlotte then successfully applied for a trainee accountancy post at a local computer company, and Joe had been placed in full-time nursery until he started school. Angie, Laura and Katy had all played a supportive role in helping with Joe, as Charlotte gradually became more independent. Nevertheless, Angie had been surprised at the strength of her daughter's self-reliance. Ollie was a regular customer at the business where Charlotte worked, and they had started dating when Joe was three. Charlotte and Joe had moved in with Ollie shortly after Joe's fourth birthday, but her friendship with Laura and Katy had remained strong.

Katy had taken the lead in organising the hen weekend and had telephoned Angie several times to run over the details. Charlotte's group of friends would all book into the hotel and spa during the afternoon, whilst Angie and one more 'older' female work colleague were invited to arrive at 7 pm for the evening meal. When Martin dropped Angie off at the hotel, Katy greeted her with a sash on which were written the words 'mother of the bride'. "You have to wear this," Katy instructed Angie.

When Angie entered the private dining room, Charlotte rushed over to her carrying a giant inflated penis-shaped balloon and a large sugary cocktail. "Hold this, Mum." She handed the balloon to Angie, and Laura took a photo.

"That's one for Facebook!" announced Laura. "Come and sit down, Angie." Angie was introduced to Margaret, a lady in her fifties who ran the accounts department. Margaret grabbed a bottle of wine and poured Angie a drink.

"I think we have been put in the 'old' corner," whispered Margaret.

"I certainly feel old," agreed Angie. "It could be a very long evening."

As the food was served, Angie watched the room of young women drinking cocktails and enjoying each other's company.

Every now and then, one of them would show the others a YouTube video on their mobile phone, and the group would explode with laughter. When the main course arrived, Charlotte walked over to her mother and asked, "Isn't this a great evening? Are you having fun?"

"Oh yes," replied Angie. When Charlotte was out of earshot, she whispered to Margaret, "What time are you leaving?"

"I'm going to ring for a taxi after dessert."

"Where do you live?"

"Bexhill."

"We'll give you a lift home."

Just after 10 pm Angie and Margaret agreed that it was late enough for them to politely depart. Angie phoned Martin, "Come and rescue us," and then said her farewells to Katy and Laura and her drunken daughter. "Enjoy the rest of your weekend. I would stay later, but Margaret has to get home, so we've offered her a lift." Charlotte hugged her mother. As Angie stepped outside to watch out for Martin, Margaret went over to Charlotte and hugged her.

"Sorry, I would stay later, but your mum needed to get home." Martin got out of Angie's car and opened the rear door for Margaret.

"Was it a good evening, ladies?"

"Like watching paint dry," admitted Angie, "but the youngsters enjoyed it, still are, and that's what matters. They didn't have many hen nights when I was Charlotte's age, only stag nights. Tonight was a bit of a mystery."

"That's equality for you," said Martin.

Margaret laughed. "Watch out for a giant inflated penis on Facebook!" Martin wanted to ask, but didn't dare. When they dropped Margaret off at her house, Martin got out of the car and walked Margaret to her front door. Her husband opened the door. Margaret felt a pang of envy as she watched Martin push his grey hair away from his eyes and walk back to Angie's car. They really were an impressive couple. "I can see why Charlotte is so self-assured," she observed to her husband.

CHAPTER THIRTY-SIX

Supply Teaching

Joe returned to school after the October half-term to discover the deputy head teacher in his classroom. She explained that his teacher was unwell but should return later in the week. The deputy head was popular so the class settled down to work without undue anxiety. Later in the day, the head teacher came into their classroom and spoke privately to the deputy head. She then addressed the class. "Dolphins, eyes towards me, please." The children sat up and looked at their head teacher. "Miss Simmons tells me that you have worked very hard today, so well done! The good news is that your own teacher, Mr Philips, is much better and will be back on Wednesday. This means you will have a supply teacher tomorrow." The class groaned. A hand went up. "Yes, Sophie?"

"Who will we have, Mrs Talbot?"

"I'm afraid I don't know yet, but whoever it is, I expect you all to behave tomorrow. It depends who the agency send. I'll be watching your class to make sure you are all polite to the visiting teacher."

Joe raised his hand. "Yes, Joe?"

"You could ask my Grandpa Martin. He's a supply teacher."

"It's a bit short notice for that now, Joe, but thank you for the suggestion. Does your Grandpa Martin live in Bexhill?"

"Sometimes. He's my grandma's boyfriend."

The class burst out laughing.

"That's enough, Dolphins," instructed Miss Simmons. "Now let's see which table is quietest, before we tidy up." The children fell into silence, while Mrs Talbot returned to her office and put on her coat. She walked outside to where the year two parents were waiting to collect their children. She spotted Angie on her own by a fence. The younger parents tended to ignore the occasional grandparent who came to pick up the children. "Mrs Stewart, can I have a word?"

"Is Joe in trouble?"

"No of course not, he's always delightful. I just wanted to ask you something. I hope you don't mind. Joe mentioned someone called Grandpa Martin, who does supply teaching?"

Angie looked embarrassed. "Well, we've never asked Joe to call him Grandpa. He just chose to do so."

"Children soon sort out who's who in a family. About the supply?"

"Martin was Head of English at Eastbourne High. He retired a couple of years ago, but now does mainly primary supply in Eastbourne. He's on the books at Eastbourne Primary."

"Thank you, Mrs Stewart. I was just being nosy really."

The children began to emerge from their classroom, and Angie moved away from Mrs Talbot so she could collect Joe. He threw his arms around her, and they walked hand in hand towards Angie's car.

Mrs Talbot weaved her way through the parents, saying goodbye to the children and eventually reached her office. She looked up the phone number of Eastbourne Primary and made a call. "Is Penny there? It's Nicola, Head of Highfields Primary."

"I think she's with a parent, I'll have a look."

"No, she's free now, I'll put you through."

"Hi Penny, did you have a good summer?"

"Not sure I can remember that far back. Too short as always. You okay?"

"Yes, I'm just ringing up for a bit of information. D'you have a supply teacher on your books, called Martin?"

"Martin Black? Yes, why d'you ask?"

"I just wondered if he was any good?"

"Very good, popular with the children and parents and easy to work with, reliable. His national curriculum knowledge is a bit rusty, but you expect that, don't you, from supply teachers. You're not planning on pinching him, are you?"

"Only if he's local to us now. Apparently, he's living in Bexhill part-time, shacked up with one of our grandparents. I thought I might contact him to go on our books, if that's okay with you?"

"Well I never, good for him! I wondered why he was a bit elusive these days. He never said anything, the dark horse. He's very good-looking, by the way, in an older man sort of way."

"Even better. I know you can't share his details, but I'll see if I can get hold of him. Thanks for your help, Penny. I owe you one."

"You certainly do…" Mrs Talbot went into the outer office.

"Dawn, have you got time to check something for me, before you go home?"

Dawn looked at her watch. "It's only a quarter-past four, I've got another fifteen minutes yet."

"Can you print off all the emergency contact details for Joe Stewart in year two?"

"Hang on, I'll do it now." Dawn opened a screen on her computer and clicked on a name. A printed contact sheet slid out from her printer. "There you are. Problems?"

"Not at all, just want to check something." Mrs Talbot looked at the sheet. There were four contact names with numbers and addresses, Charlotte Stewart Mother, Darren Foley Father, Angela Stewart Grandmother, Oliver Manston Mother's partner, but no Martin Black. She decided to try and catch Angie again for a chat.

The following day, when Mrs Talbot was in the school playground at home-time, she spotted a tall man standing next to Angie. She watched him unconsciously sweep his hair from his forehead. Penny was right. He was extremely attractive. The children were leaving their classrooms, and she noticed Joe hurtle himself into Martin's arms. She smiled as she overheard Martin say, "No, not the red car today, Joe, you'll have to put up with Grandma's BMW."

"Mr Black?" Mrs Talbot interrupted. She held out her hand to Martin. "I'm Nicola Talbot, Head of Joe's school. You couldn't spare me five minutes, could you?"

Angie looked worried. "Should I come?"

Mrs Talbot smiled. "This is not about Joe. I just wanted to discuss something with Mr Black. You can take Joe into the library, if you like. I think the computers are still on."

"Yes…" shouted Joe. "I can show Grandma the superhero programme."

Mrs Talbot laughed. "Believe it or not that programme is educational. It's full of maths challenges." Joe pulled Angie's hand towards the library, while Martin followed Mrs Talbot to her office. Ten minutes later they walked back to the library. Martin had a broad grin on his face. "Thanks Nicola, I'll get that paperwork to you tomorrow." Martin and Angie walked towards the car, each holding Joe's hand.

"Nicola? It didn't take you long to get on first name terms."

"That's because I'm irresistible to women." Angie couldn't contain her curiosity.

"Well then, what did she want?"

"She's offered me some supply work at Joe's school, and I've accepted."

Joe interrupted, "I told her to ask you."

Angie and Martin exchanged glances.

"You don't miss much, do you, Joe?" observed Martin.

Angie gave Joe a hug. "I think you deserve a very large bag of sweets."

"And a comic?"

"And a comic," they both repeated.

CHAPTER THIRTY-SEVEN

The Accident

It was three weeks until the wedding. Alison had been growing increasingly weak and began to use an oxygen mask to help her to breathe more easily. Susan texted Angie to let her know that a move to the local hospice was imminent. Martin and Angie decided to visit Alison at the hospice the following day. Susan had indicated that her sister's likely prognosis was less than two weeks, but Angie still hoped that Alison might hang on long enough to see the wedding photos. Her skin looked very grey as they entered the room. Alison was drifting in and out of wakefulness, so Martin and Angie talked together in quiet voices. Angie's phone started to vibrate. It was a text from Charlotte.

I'm at the school. Joe's banged his head. Nothing serious but he might need a stitch. My car's in the garage. Any chance of a lift to the Conquest?

Alison opened her eyes, and Angie read her the message. Alison grabbed the paper and pen which were always present at her bedside. She wrote in a shaky hand.

ASK MARTIN TO GO I NEED YOU HERE

Angie thought she noticed Alison smile. "Martin, how would you feel about picking Charlotte and Joe up from school, then driving them to the Conquest in my car?"

"Is he hurt?"

"Just a minor bang on the head, I think, but better safe than sorry."

"Will Charlotte mind that it's me?"

"Let's find out."

Angie texted.

I'm with Alison at the hospice, but Martin will come and collect you in my car. Is that okay?

It will have to be x

Angie turned to Martin. "Charlotte's fine with it. The seat's in my car, so perhaps you could collect me on your way back from A&E? I'm very grateful." She kissed him on the cheek.

"And I feel strangely apprehensive. Tell Charlotte I'll be with her in about twenty minutes."

Angie spoke to Alison once Martin had left. "Was that wise?"

Alison pulled the oxygen mask away from her face. "Wait and see."

Martin parked in the staff car park at Joe's school. He keyed in the entry code, pressed the button and walked into the reception area. Dawn spoke to him through the hatch. "Hi, Martin, I didn't know you were working today."

"I'm not. I'm on substitute grandparent duty. Where are Charlotte and Joe? It's fallen to me to take them to A and E."

"They're in the medical room. Joe's fine in himself, but he's got a nasty cut on his chin and quite a bump. Be warned, there's blood." Dawn let Martin through. Charlotte was pacing the floor of the medical room, clutching her mobile phone. Joe was holding a dressing on his chin, but as soon as he spotted Martin, he ran towards him.

"Hey steady on, old man, bumps like that need a bit of respect." Martin scrutinised Joe's face and forehead. The chin was still bleeding, and the bump was bright red and about the size of a golf ball. "That's a very impressive size, Joe. We should take a photo to show at school tomorrow, but let's get it looked at first, shall we?" He grabbed some extra tissues, took Joe's hand and led him to the car with Charlotte following carrying Joe's school bag. "I'm not trying to worry you," he said quietly to Charlotte.

"Bumps that swell outwards are less likely to cause concussion, than the ones that don't swell as much, but just as a precaution, I think you should sit in the back with him. He also might need a stitch on his chin. Keep him awake. Don't let the motion of the car send him to sleep."

"Okay, whatever you say. How do you know this stuff?"

"I'm a qualified school first aider, Charlotte. I've got years of experience with banged heads." Martin drove carefully to the Conquest and dropped Charlotte and Joe at the entrance to A and E. "I'll park and come and join you."

When Martin arrived in A and E, he could hear a child screaming. He followed the noise to a curtained area, where Joe was stood up stamping his feet with his back to the young doctor.

Charlotte looked tearful. "I don't know what to do. He's refusing to let the doctor examine him."

Martin walked over to Joe. "Hi Joe, look what I found in Grandma's car." Joe kept facing the wall but stopped yelling.

"What?"

"Turn round, and I'll show you." Joe slowly turned round and looked at Martin's clenched hand. "Shh… it's magic and very shy. Come and sit next to me and I'll show you, but you have to whisper."

Charlotte and the doctor watched in admiration as Joe sat next to Martin, who spoke in a very soft voice. He slowly opened his fingers. "It's an invisible magic superhero. It will only turn into a real one if you are very, very brave."

"A real what?"

"Superhero. Who's your favourite?"

"Spiderman," whispered Joe.

Martin lifted his hand to his ear and pretended to listen. "Spiderman says, he will become a real toy later, but only if you are a very, very brave boy."

"Okay," whispered Joe. "Will it hurt?"

"The hospital has special superpower spray, Joe. It takes away the hurt." The doctor began to examine Joe's head, while Martin continued to talk to him. Joe allowed the doctor to spray his chin with an analgesic coating before sticking his wound together with strips and adding a dressing.

The doctor spoke. "Joe, follow my finger with your eyes. No, don't move your head. Good boy, do you feel dizzy or sick?"

"I just feel brave," declared Joe, "like Spiderman!" Joe stood up and started to pretend to climb the wall.

"Joe, you mustn't run around," instructed Martin. "The dressing might come off, and we haven't taken a photo yet to show Grandma?"

The doctor spoke. "Thank you for your help. Young children aren't really my thing. Keep an eye out for any signs of concussion and bring him straight back if you notice anything." The doctor handed Charlotte a leaflet. "This will explain what to look for. Don't let him sleep for at least another two hours, and make sure someone is with him to keep an eye out tonight. No school tomorrow, but after that he can go back."

Charlotte blinked back the tears. "Thank you, Doctor. Joe, say thank you to the doctor."

Joe did as he was asked. "Thank you." He turned to Martin. "Is it time to fetch the Spiderman toy now?"

Martin looked at his watch. "It'll have to wait until tomorrow, Joe, but a promise is a promise. You will get a Spiderman for being so brave, as long as that's okay with Mummy."

Charlotte smiled. "Of course it is, and maybe we can take that photo in the waiting area?" Martin sat Joe on a chair and took his photo.

"D'you want a copy for Ollie?" he asked Charlotte. She nodded. "I'm just going to text your mum to put her mind at rest and then I'll send it to you, but I'll need your number. D'you want to see, Joe?"

Joe looked at the photo of his face. "Wow! I was brave."

"I'll bring the car round," he said to Charlotte. "Stay in the warm and watch out for me."

They were soon driving back to the hospice with Joe happily chatting to his mother in the back of the car. Angie was waiting outside and climbed into the passenger seat. Reassured that Joe was okay, she asked Charlotte, "D'you want to come back to mine, or go home?"

"It must be home. Ollie will want to see Joe."

"Can Grandpa Martin come too?"

Martin answered, "I have to search for Spiderman, Joe, but hopefully Grandma and I might pop in and see you tomorrow, if that's okay with Mummy?"

Charlotte answered, "Of course you can, Martin." It was the first time she had ever addressed him by his name. When Angie and Martin finally returned to her flat, they stood on the balcony and enjoyed the sunset. "What exactly went on in A and E, Martin? And what's all this about Spiderman?"

"Joe was a bit upset at first, that's all. It was nothing that couldn't be solved by a bit of Martin magic and a touch of bribery. I need to go on Amazon later and find an express delivery."

"Is this something I should pay for?"

"Certainly not."

CHAPTER THIRTY-EIGHT

The Secret

Martin was overwhelmed with relief that he had finally, so he believed, made a connection with Charlotte. He spent the evening searching online for a toy Spiderman and eventually found one with batteries, which he could 'click and collect' the following day. Angie was visiting a client, so he went alone to pick up the toy, then went straight to Charlotte and Ollie's house to deliver his parcel. He felt disappointed when there was no reply, and he had to leave the parcel in their porch. With a call from Joe's school for him to do an emergency afternoon's supply, he had no time to dwell on his disappointment. Back at the flat after work, he received a text from an unknown number.

Hi Martin, Ollie here. Joe was made up with his Spiderman. Re wedding Charlotte and I need a chat without Angie knowing. When and where would suit?

Martin felt a mixture of pleasure and nervousness. He hoped all was well, but was delighted that he had been taken into their confidence. He texted back.

I'm working tomorrow, but free any other day. Angie is seeing a client on Friday, so I could meet you easily then.

The reply was immediate.

Friday then. 11am ours?

Agreed.

That Friday in November, less than two weeks before the date of Charlotte and Ollie's wedding, Martin stood at the entrance to their house and rang the bell. The door opened immediately, and Charlotte led Martin into their open plan kitchen/living room. Martin sat down. "This is nice." He accepted Ollie's offer of coffee, and they spent the next fifteen minutes sorting out who drank what, with or without milk and sugar until they were finally all seated with a drink. Ollie looked at Charlotte. "Do you want to ask?"

"No, you do it."

Ollie spoke. "Martin, I don't want to go over the past, but Charlotte and I feel we weren't always very fair to you."

"You were fair, Ollie," interrupted Charlotte. "This wasn't your fault."

"Anyway," continued Ollie, "we are grateful that you didn't give up on us, and we owe you a lot." Ollie paused. "There's something we want to ask you, but we will understand if you say no." Martin felt uneasy, but stayed silent.

Charlotte took over. "I was wondering if you would agree to give me away at the wedding?" For once Martin was speechless.

"Well?" Ollie asked.

Martin finally spoke. "I would be honoured."

"The snag is that you'll need a morning suit fitted, and we thought we might keep it a secret from Mum until our wedding. It would really surprise her."

"You can say that again," agreed Martin. "So when's the fitting? And do I need a rehearsal?"

"Jess promised she'd talk you through it, and the fitting is tomorrow, if you can make it."

"Quite a conspiracy," mumbled Martin. "What time tomorrow and where? You haven't left me much time to concoct a story to stop Angie getting suspicious."

Ollie turned to Martin. "I thought I could ring you this evening and invite you round tomorrow to help with my speech?"

"That's a good plan. And, er, talking of speeches, do you want one from me?"

Charlotte replied, "Maybe just a few words?"

As Martin was about to leave, Ollie put his hand on Martin's shoulder. "I know Charlotte isn't family, but we were wondering if there was anyone you'd like us to invite? I mean you're taking a major role now. Maybe we should ask the other cousins that Angie mentioned."

"That's really not necessary. I hardly ever see them these days, and I will have Jess there."

"Well, if you think of anyone..."

Martin hesitated. "There is someone Angie would really like to come."

"Who's that, then?"

"Carly, the girl who made all the wedding flowers. Apparently, she's never been to a wedding."

Charlotte interrupted. "Never been to a wedding, at her age! How odd! Yes, it would be lovely if she could come. Do you have her address?"

Martin hoped he had done the right thing. "If you give me the invite, I'm sure Angie would like to deliver it." By the time Martin reached the flat, with the invitation for Carly in his pocket, his head was buzzing. He arrived just in time to read a text from Charlotte.

Have not told Joe. Don't think he could keep the secret.

Martin re-read the text and then deleted it.

The following day, after Martin had returned from his suit fitting, Angie received a call from Alison's sister. "She's deteriorating fast. You might want to visit." Angie immediately told Martin, and he fetched the car keys. Within half an hour they were sitting beside Alison's bed in the hospice. Susan beckoned Angie outside for a chat, leaving Martin alone with Alison. Her mouth was still covered by an oxygen mask, but Martin could see Alison's eyes moving. He drew his face close to Alison's and whispered, "Charlotte has asked me to give her away at the wedding. It's a secret. Don't tell Angie."

Alison pulled away the oxygen mask and spoke quietly, "That's bloody brilliant."

Angie and Susan returned to the room, and Martin tactfully left them alone with Alison. Some time later he could hear an alarm sounding from Alison's bedside. She had died with her sister and her best friend each holding her hand.

CHAPTER THIRTY-NINE

Farewell to Eastbourne

In the days following Alison's death, Angie hardly slept. Martin would find her sitting in the kitchen drinking Earl Grey tea with a box of tissues in front of her. He knew it would need time for Angie to pick herself up after losing such a close friend, but he was worried that she had taken it so hard. On the fourth sleepless night he got dressed and joined her in the kitchen. Angie looked at Martin with tears running down her cheeks. "I'm sorry. I can't seem to pull myself out of this."

Martin sat down and took her hand. "It will take time, Angie, I know that, but I am worried about you. If you can't shake off the depths of your grief, you won't enjoy Charlotte's wedding." He risked a joke. "And you'll ruin the wedding photos, if you look miserable."

Angie managed a smile. "The problem is I keep dreaming about her. She's haunting my sleep. Last night I dreamt Alison was at Charlotte's wedding wearing an oxygen mask and screaming at me, because I had forgotten to connect her to the drip. It was a terrible dream. I was relieved to wake up."

Martin kissed Angie's forehead. "You've had too much emotional stuff come at you at the same time. It's hardly surprising that you're struggling to cope. At least Alison insisted that the funeral must take place before the wedding. That might help a bit."

Angie tried hard to be positive. "Whatever you do, don't tell Carly about the funeral."

Martin suddenly stood up. "Which reminds me, I've got some news about Carly. With everything that happened I completely forgot to tell you." He went into the hall and retrieved an envelope from his coat pocket. "I hope I've done the right thing. I've got an invitation for Carly to come to the wedding." Martin handed the envelope to Angie, and she pulled out the oyster-coloured card.

Charlotte and Ollie request the presence of Carly Smith at the celebration of their wedding...

The idea of Carly coming to the wedding seemed to lift Angie out of her depression. "This is such a lovely idea. How on earth did you persuade them to invite her?"

"There's nothing the Martin charm can't achieve." He squeezed Angie's hand. "Actually, I simply asked, and they said yes." He pulled Angie to her feet. "Come on, we're going out. Go and get dressed."

"Where?"

"My house in Eastbourne. I need some clothes for the wedding... and Alison's funeral."

It was dark when Martin used the remote control to open Angie's garage. He still felt a guilty pleasure when he sat in the driving seat of her BMW. She climbed in beside him and fastened her seat belt. He noticed she pulled a lipstick from her bag and added some colour to her lips, a good sign, he reflected, that the former elegant Angie had not completely disappeared.

The roads were empty, and it took less than half an hour to reach Martin's house. He found a space on the road, and they both got out of the car. Martin unlocked the front door and they entered the house. "God, it's cold in here." Martin turned up the thermostat.

"It smells musty, too," said Angie. "It's not good to leave a house empty for too long."

Martin made a suggestion. "There's a café down the road. It's a bit rough, but it opens early. Shall we go there now for breakfast? Give the house time to warm up?"

Angie nodded in agreement. "Good idea."

They wrapped up warmly and walked to the café hand in hand. They could smell brewing coffee as they approached the door. Angie was hungry for the first time since Alison's death. Martin felt relieved, as he watched her tuck into a large plate of bacon and eggs. "How are you going to tell Carly about the wedding invite? Will you ring her?"

Angie looked up. "I was supposed to collect the flowers last week, but it got delayed because of Alison. I really must ring her to arrange to fetch them. I've never actually been inside her bedsit, but if she invites me in, I can discuss it then. She's bound to be nervous about it. You'll keep an eye on her at the wedding, won't you?"

"Of course I will, and I'm sure we can find someone of her own age to look after her, if we're busy." Martin thought carefully about his choice of words.

"D'you think she'd let me buy her something to wear?" Angie asked.

"She's proud, but you could probably persuade her," Martin replied. He could see that the idea of supporting Carly was helping to distract Angie from her grief.

When the couple returned to the house, it was much warmer. Martin showed Angie into the spare bedroom and opened the wardrobe door. He pulled out the dark suit which he had worn for Jack's funeral. "I know it sounds a bit crass, but I thought this might do for both the wedding and the funeral." Angie felt slightly disappointed. She had hoped to buy Martin a new suit for the wedding. "Will it still fit?"

"Should do, I could do with a new shirt though, for the wedding, I mean. I'll need your help choosing." Martin sensed that Angie would not be happy unless he bought something new.

"I don't want to do it today, but we could go into Hastings at the weekend." He pulled a selection of ties out from a drawer and put the black one in his pocket. Angie examined the rest and scowled. Martin sighed. "Okay, I'll buy a new tie as well." He hoped he might be able to keep the receipt and take the tie back, once Angie realised he wouldn't need it. They carried the suit, together with a white shirt for the funeral, downstairs. Angie sat on the settee.

"I don't want to go back to the flat quite yet. It's done me good to get away for a while." She felt the need to make conversation. "Are you still enjoying your supply work at Joe's school?"

"I love it, and Nicola says that there's another nearby school interested as well, not that I want to work full-time, but it's so much easier, now I don't have to travel from Bexhill to Eastbourne."

"Don't you miss living here? Having your own place?"

Martin was aware of the opportunity to address an, as yet, unexplored topic. "I don't miss this place at all. I much prefer living with you in Bexhill."

"You did say once that you felt the central maintenance and the management committee rather intrusive."

Martin laughed. "I did at first, but I've gradually settled into the place. And since that encounter with Frank, I've sort of become a bit of a local hero. People keep stopping me in the lobby and telling me what a pain he was. It seems we weren't the only ones he was upsetting."

Angie stood up and walked around Martin's house. "If I helped you do this place up, it would fetch a good rent... and provide you with some extra income."

Martin looked surprised. "It never occurred to me to rent it out. That's a brilliant idea, but it would mean you couldn't get rid of me." He took Angie in his arms. "This would be a big commitment."

"Actually, not that big, because you would still own the house and could let it out on a short-term lease."

Martin held her gaze. "I'm not afraid of commitment, Angie. I want to live with you permanently." He gave her a questioning look. "As long as this isn't a knee-jerk reaction to losing Alison."

"I've been thinking about it for ages, just didn't like to say. It would help our relationship too, if you had some extra income, and we would only have one set of bills between us. I know you find it difficult me having more money than you."

Martin did an internet search on his phone. "Blimey, I didn't realise rents in Eastbourne were so high!"

Angie began to plan. "You'd be better to let it unfurnished, but you'd have to get rid of a lot of stuff."

"And I doubt anyone would want most of my old junk. Am I allowed to keep the TV?"

Angie sighed. "I think it would look great on the wall in my living room, sorry, our living room."

They turned the heating down and drove back to Bexhill filled with the promise of a more secure future together. Angie knew her sadness would return, but it had temporarily been buried under her plans with Martin. They discussed their new project in the car. "I think we should give Carly first refusal on your stuff, unless Jess would want any of it."

"I wouldn't insult her by offering."

"Has Jess got a boyfriend?" Angie suddenly asked. "She never mentions anyone."

"It's not the sort of information she tends to share with her old dad in detail, but there doesn't seem to have been anyone serious for ages. I think she was a bit put off the whole relationship thing when her mum chucked me out. Having said that, I've noticed a change in her recently. She's got a bit of her old sparkle back, and she's taking great care over her appearance. At first, I thought it was just the new job, but I do think she might have found someone."

"She's extremely attractive, like her father." The car pulled into the garage, and the conversation about Jessica was closed.

CHAPTER FORTY

TV and Flowers

The day after Martin and Angie had returned from Eastbourne, Angie phoned Carly on her mobile. "Hello?"

"Carly, I'm sorry it's taken me so long to get back to you. Can I come over today and collect the wedding flowers?"

Carly sounded a little apprehensive. "You want to come here?"

"Well, you don't drive, and I doubt that you could carry them to my flat."

"Oh yes, of course. When d'you want to come?"

"Would this afternoon be okay?" Once a time was agreed, Carly began to clean and tidy her already clean and tidy bedsit. At 2 pm Angie rang her doorbell, and Carly buzzed her in.

"It's the top floor." Angie climbed the stairs, and Carly was waiting for her. She stepped inside the bedsit and glanced around.

"This is lovely. It reminds me of the bedsit I had when I was a student."

Carly's response surprised her. "But I'm not a student. I'm a grown woman with my own business, and this is all I can afford."

Angie thought hard before replying, "I don't want to patronise you, Carly, but you haven't exactly had it easy. I think you have achieved a great deal." Carly produced three plastic boxes full of flowers wrapped in tissue paper.

"I can't unwrap them all, but I will show you the bouquet." She carefully pulled out the bridal bouquet and laid it on her bed. The combination of irises, white peonies and silver honesty, all delicately hand-stitched, was exquisite. Angie found tears running down her cheeks. Carly sounded anxious. "Don't you like them?"

"Carly, they are so beautiful, perfect. I'm sorry. My best friend died last week, and I'm still very emotional, but these are tears of pure joy." Carly grabbed a piece of kitchen roll, and handed it to Angie.

"Can I make you a cup of tea?"

Angie blew her nose. "That would be lovely."

While the kettle was boiling, Angie looked round the bedsit. "Do you have a TV?"

"It's been on my list of things to buy for ages. There is an aerial point, and I've been saving up for a licence."

"I've got a TV I don't want. Would you like it?"

Carly pulled a doubtful face. "I don't take charity. I've had too many do-gooders in my life. Sorry, I don't mean to offend you. There was a time when I would take anything from anyone, but I'm learning to be independent." Angie took her mug of tea and thought carefully about her choice of words.

"Carly, you know Martin, the man who sometimes lives with me?"

"The good-looking one, yes. He seems kind."

"He is kind, and he's going to move in with me permanently. He's bringing this bloody great TV with him, and I already have a TV in every room, so you can have the one from my living room. I really don't need it."

"Can't you sell it?"

"Second-hand TVs fetch very little these days. It's not worth selling it, and you can have first pick of anything from Martin's house too. The rest will just go to the tip. This is not charity. It will save us work, and I don't like to see things go to waste." Carly hesitated, and Angie continued, "Please, Carly, I've had such a shit week, and I would like to feel I've achieved something positive."

Carly smiled. "I can't really refuse then, can I?"

"Good. Martin and I will arrange to take you to Eastbourne a few days after the wedding, but you can have the TV as soon as he has delivered that monster of his to my flat, I should say our flat, but I keep forgetting."

Carly smiled. "Thank you."

"Actually, there's more to say," continued Angie. "I think I'd better just come out with it. Charlotte and Ollie would like you to come to the wedding. I have an invitation for you."

It was Carly's turn to look tearful. "I'd love to come, but what on earth could I wear? I don't think my black suit would do." Angie decided that Carly had received as much generosity as she could cope with in one day.

"I'm sure we can think of something, Carly. You're about the same size and age as my Charlotte. She might have something she doesn't want anymore, and you're good with a needle if anything needs altering." Angie hoped Carly was not offended. "Come on, let's get these boxes down to my car."

CHAPTER FORTY-ONE

Farewell to Alison

Martin was finding it increasingly difficult to hide his new wedding role from Angie. He had to fabricate a story to explain the need to drive to the hotel in separate cars. Angie very reluctantly agreed to drive Joe and Carly in her car, so Martin could leave earlier and journey into work with Jessica. Angie didn't like the arrangement but did see the point of them only having one car at the hotel, so they could travel home together the following day. Martin was almost grateful that Alison's funeral was so close to the wedding and distracting Angie's thoughts. They woke early on the morning of the funeral, and Martin got dressed in his black suit and tie. Angie looked at the suit jacket and shook her head. "It is a bit tight, Martin. You really should have bought a new suit for the wedding."

"It's your fault for over-feeding me. It's too late now anyway. No one will notice. They'll all be looking at your hat." Angie felt too emotional to argue.

Angie drove to the crematorium in Hastings. She was surprised that so many people had gathered to be part of the send-off for her friend. Susan greeted them and made sure they were seated near the front. Angie had agreed to read a poem, which she gripped in a cardboard folder. As the coffin was carried into the chapel,

Angie felt herself welling up. The tears began to stream down her face. The minister gave a well-researched tribute to Alison and mentioned Angie as her closest friend. He expressed Susan's thanks for Angie's support during Alison's final weeks. When it was Angie's turn to read, she mumbled, "I don't think I can do this."

"Yes, you can," insisted Martin. "You're putting on a show for Alison. Come on, I'll stand beside you."

He took her hand and led her to the front of the chapel. He put his arm round her shoulder and held the words in front of her. "Take a very deep breath," he instructed. She breathed in and read the poem in a clear and fluent voice. Martin led her back to her seat. "Well done, love." He passed her a packet of tissues. "Now you can cry as much as you want." And she did.

There was a short gathering afterwards at a church hall across the road. Everyone felt relieved that the funeral was over. Martin took Angie's hand and led her to the table of food. "I'm not hungry," she protested.

"I don't want you to eat. I just want to show you something."

There at the centre of the table was a plate of egg sandwiches and a dish of sausage rolls.

"You see, we should have invited Carly." They both burst into laughter, releasing much of the emotion from the funeral. Martin insisted on driving home, and the size of his suit was not discussed again before the wedding. With only two days to go, Angie phoned Carly on their return. She agreed a time to pick her up, and asked about her wedding outfit.

"You don't have to worry," Carly reassured Angie. "I picked up the perfect dress and shoes at one of the charity shops in Bexhill."

"Nobody wants my help with clothes for this wedding," Angie grumbled to herself.

CHAPTER FORTY-TWO

My Daughter's Wedding

The day of the wedding finally arrived. Joe had stayed overnight at the flat and woke very early in excitement. Martin went downstairs and hung his suit and shirt in the back of his Fiat. He returned to say goodbye to Joe and Angie, then left early as pre-arranged, having told Angie he would be meeting Jessica in Eastbourne. He headed west along the seafront in case Angie was watching, then, once out of sight, circled north to turn back to Ollie and Charlotte's house. Charlotte and the bridesmaids had stayed at Belmont Grange the night before, so Martin was greeted by Ollie and Mike. Three adult morning suits were hanging on a clothes rail in the living room, together with an identical smaller suit for Joe. "Aww," said Martin, "there won't be a dry eye in the place."

"Was Joe okay this morning?" asked Ollie.

"Up early, very excited, but otherwise fine. Angie was still a bit miffed at having to drive herself and Joe to the hotel, but she wouldn't dare have a go at me in front of Joe. Joe was threatened with a lifelong sweets ban, if he sat on Angie's hat by mistake." All three men found themselves pacing the floor.

"We might as well go soon," said Ollie to Martin. "We need to arrive well before Angie, so we can hide you away. Does anyone mind if I have a beer first?"

"You carry on, mate," said Mike. "I can't as I'm driving."

"And I'm not starting this early," grinned Martin. Ollie drained the beer glass at speed, and the three men climbed into Mike's car.

Jessica was watching for them when they arrived. She instructed a member of staff to carry the morning suits up to the best man's room and hugged her father. "Are you okay? Has Angie guessed?"

"She hasn't a clue, though she doesn't approve of my choice of suit. It was just as well she had Alison's funeral to distract her."

"Sorry, Dad, I forgot to ask. Did it go okay?"

Martin shrugged. "As expected."

Martin stared at his daughter. "You look absolutely lovely, Jess."

"Thanks, Dad." He thought he noticed her blush. "Now we'd better get you out of the way in case Angie arrives. I've arranged for Laura to come down and fetch Joe, in case Angie tries to take him upstairs."

"She'll wonder where I am."

"I'll think of something," reassured Jessica.

Once in the hotel room, the three men began to get changed into their morning suits. Four hand-sewn buttonholes were laid on a table next to a bottle of champagne on ice. They clipped the buttonholes to their suits and admired themselves in the long mirror. "We brush up okay, don't we?" said Ollie. "The official photographer is with Charlotte, but we ought to have a photo too."

"I'll ask Jess if she's got time to do it." Martin texted her with the request.

Can't, busy. Will send someone.

A few minutes later there was a knock on the door. An expensively-dressed man in his mid-thirties came in. "Hi, I'm Philip Walsh, Kenton Walsh's son. Which of you is the groom?"

"Me," Ollie stepped forward, and Philip shook his hand warmly. "Congratulations. You all look great."

He turned towards Mike. "So you must be the best man. Is everything okay so far? You will let me know if you need anything?"

"It's all fine so far," answered Mike gratefully.

Philip looked at Martin. "And I don't have to ask who you are. Jess obviously takes after her father." Philip shook Martin's hand. Ollie thought Philip looked slightly embarrassed. "Champagne," stuttered Philip. "It's on the house. Would you like me to open it for you?"

"Yes please," agreed Mike. Philip filled three glasses and asked for everyone's phones to take some photos. Then, somewhat surprisingly, took out his own phone and took a photo. "I thought I'd show Jess," he explained. There was a tap on the door, and Laura appeared holding Joe's hand.

"Grandpa Martin," screamed Joe. "You look very posh!"

"What about me?" complained Ollie.

"You too, Ollie," and he gave his future stepfather a hug.

"Shall I get him changed in the bathroom?" asked Laura.

"Please do," replied Ollie, "and thank you!"

"I have to warn you, Martin," continued Laura, "Angie is down there with Carly, and she kept asking where you are. Jess fobbed her off with a story about you fixing a broken table. It was such a stupid excuse that Angie believed it."

"How was Carly?"

"Looking very smart in a pale blue dress. It must have cost a fortune." Martin smiled. A few minutes later Laura led Joe out of the bathroom wearing his morning suit. Martin knelt down and attached the buttonhole to his jacket.

"Now," he said, "you must be a very good boy and keep this suit clean."

"I'm a bit frightened, Martin," whispered Joe.

"No need, little man. I've brought the magic superhero with me. He's pinned to your suit with the flower."

Joe stroked the buttonhole and smiled. "Thanks, Grandpa Martin." Seeing that Joe was settled, Laura rushed off to Charlotte's room to change into her bridesmaid dress.

"One more photo, I think," said Philip, and Joe joined the group in their morning suits. Photos taken, Philip shook Martin's hand.

"Good to meet you, sir." He left the room.

It was fifteen minutes before the ceremony was due to start. The guests were ushered into The Orangery. Angie looked stunning in her extravagantly-trimmed hat with the matching hand-sewn buttonhole fixed to her jacket. She and Carly sat in the front row, leaving a space between them for Martin. The registrar entered with his assistant and set out the papers on the large ornate table. Jessica walked into the room and approached Angie. "Dad said not to worry, he'll be with you in a minute."

"He's cutting it a bit fine," she tutted. Then Ollie and Mike entered the room and sat on the chairs which had been allocated for them. The guests spoke in hushed tones while they waited for something to happen. Angie looked round the room, but there was still no sign of Martin. She spotted Jessica peer through the rear door and nod to the registrar.

A voice announced, "Will you please be upstanding to welcome the bride."

A recording played Pachelbel's *Canon*, and everybody stood. Ollie looked nervously towards the door. Laura and Katy appeared first, each holding one of Joe's hands. Joe was grinning broadly and, as they walked past Angie, he pulled one of his hands away and frantically waved at his grandma. "Look," he mouthed at her and pointed behind. Angie was stunned as she realised Joe was pointing at Martin dressed in a morning suit. Charlotte was holding his arm. She put her hand over her mouth and gasped. The bridesmaids and Joe sat down, while Martin handed Charlotte over to Ollie and then took his own seat next to Angie. "Sorry I'm late," he whispered. She shook her head and tried to concentrate on the wedding. The music stopped and the ceremony began. Joe sat perfectly still between the two bridesmaids with one hand on his superhero buttonhole while he watched his mother and Ollie declare their love for each other. Angie finally heard the words 'I now pronounce you husband and wife' and held onto Martin's hand as she tried to control her tears. Carly looked around the room and wondered if she could design a complete floral package for a wedding. Martin, however, found himself distracted. Tucked into a far corner of the room he spotted Philip Walsh with his arm around Jessica. Could it be that the heir to the Kenward empire was in a relationship with his daughter? He tried to set aside his curiosity, as they finally filed out of The Orangery and entered the dining room. Carly was seated on a table between two of Charlotte's friends, whilst Angie found herself on the top table with Joe and Martin on either side.

"My two favourite men," she whispered to Martin.

The speeches were timetabled between the main course and the dessert. The wine had been flowing, and the glasses were now filled with champagne. Ollie spoke first and thanked everyone who had helped with the organisation of the wedding. He told Charlotte how beautiful she looked, praised Joe for his good behaviour, and gave a special mention to Carly and the exquisite hand-sewn flowers. This produced a loud cheer from the guests, and Carly found herself blushing. Ollie finished by presenting Angie with a bouquet of real flowers. It was then Mike's turn. He told several embarrassing anecdotes about Ollie, and the room filled with laughter. He then toasted the bridesmaids and Joe. Laura and Katy were given gifts wrapped in white paper and decorated with purple ribbon. Joe was presented with a large box, wrapped in brightly-coloured superhero paper.

"Can I open it now?" Joe whispered to Angie.

"You certainly can, Joe." She took off her jacket and laid it on the floor. "You've been sat at the table long enough. Sit down there and open your present. You can come back up when the puddings arrive."

Carly left her table and walked over to Angie. "Do you think I could watch Joe open his present?"

"Of course, Carly." And Carly sat on the floor next to Joe to soak up a borrowed family experience which had been so lacking in her own life.

It had been agreed that Martin would speak last, and, at the allotted time, he rose to his feet. Not having the right to talk about Charlotte as his daughter, he had already decided to keep his speech short. He sincerely thanked the couple for allowing him the privilege of giving Charlotte away, and then added how much he appreciated Ollie's help in looking after him so well at the stag 'do'. This raised laughter from several of the younger guests. Martin pointed out that he was not an expert himself at creating a successful marriage. At this point Ollie shouted, "There's still time, Martin!" and, much to Angie's embarrassment, there was a spontaneous round of applause. Martin grinned and then spoke warmly about the young couple and their obvious love for each other. He asked the guests to stand for a toast to the bride and groom. The wedding guests then sat down, assuming that the speeches had finished, but Martin called them to order. "I would just like to say one more thing." The room fell silent. "There are several people who we would have loved to share today's wedding, but they are unable to be with us. However, I am convinced that they are looking down on us and sending their love from a better place." Ollie thought of his parents and brother, Charlotte thought of her father, and Angie thought of Alison. Martin handed her a tissue. "So, I would like to propose one final toast... to absent friends."

The wedding guests rose and picked up their glasses.

"To absent friends."